Praise for **SUCKS TO BE ME**

An ALA Quick Pick for Reluctant Young Adult Readers

"Great concept, great character, great fun."
   —Sarah Mlynowski, author of *Bras and Broomsticks*

"It's rare for a writer to come up with a new and original twist on vampirism, but in *Sucks to Be Me* Kimberly Pauley has done just that. The novel's biting wit and keen portrayal of teenage angst will make it a sure hit."
   —E. Rose Sabin, author of *School for Sorcery*

"Though I don't normally read vampire books, I was sucked right in by the hilarious yet sweet voice of Mina in *Sucks to Be Me* . . . The only thing that sucks about this book is that it had to end. A great read!"
   —D. L. Garfinkle, author of *Storky* and *Stuck in the 70's*

"*Sucks To Be Me* puts a sweet, funny twist on the usual teen vampire story. The concept is inventive and the characters are a lot of fun."
   —Susan Juby, author of *Alice, I Think*

"[This book] literally made me snort lemonade through my nose! Pauley dares to go there again and again, with topical references and jabs at modern-day vampire lore. Her main character is a self-described closet girly-girl who has kick-butt tendencies and an attitude that readers will love. Totally entertaining, with a top-of-the-line teen voice!"
   —Julie M. Prince, Teenreadstoo.com (5 stars)

"The lively pace, amusing tone, and accessibly non-gory vampire plot make this an ideal summer beach r̶ ̶̶ ̶articularly for horror fans who may appreciate a lighter l̶ ̶ ̶ ̶ ̶ ̶h toward immortal bloodsucker."
   —*Bulletin o̶̶ ̶ ̶ ̶ ̶ ̶ ̶ ̶ ̶ Books*

"The adolescent vam̶ ̶ ̶ ̶ ̶ ̶ ̶ ̶ ̶ ̶ ̶ ̶̶rrely heartwarming treatme̶ ̶ ̶ ̶ ̶ ̶ ̶ ̶ ̶ ̶ ̶ual mix, a welcome change from al̶ ̶ ̶ ̶ ̶ ̶ ̶ ̶ ̶vampire novels around these days, and a v̶ ̶ ̶ ̶ ̶ ̶ ̶ ̶novel."
   —*Locus*

SUCKS
TO BE ME

The ALL-TRUE
confessions of
MINA HAMILTON,
Teen Vampire MAYBE

Kimberly Pauley

MIRRORSTONE®

Sucks to Be Me
The All-True Confessions of Mina Hamilton, Teen Vampire (Maybe)
©2009 by Kimberly Pauley

Published by Wizards of the Coast LLC

Mirrorstone and its logo are trademarks of Wizards of the Coast LLC in the U.S.A. and other countries.

Printed in the U.S.A.

Art by Emi Tanji
Cover photo by Allison Shinkle
Book designed by Emi Tanji and Kate Irwin

First Printing

9 8 7 6 5 4 3 2 1

ISBN: 978-0-7869-5256-4
620-24230000-001-EN

The Library of Congress has catalogued the hardcover edition as follows:

Pauley, Kimberly, 1973-
  Sucks to be me : the all-true confessions of Mina Hamilton, teen vampire (maybe) / by Kimberly Pauley.
    p. cm.
  "Mirrorstone."
  Summary: When sixteen-year-old Mina is forced to take a class to help her decide whether or not to become a vampire like her parents, she also faces a choice between her life-long best friend and the boy she has a crush on versus new friends and possible boyfriends in her mandatory "vampire lessons."
  ISBN 978-0-7869-5028-7
  [1. Vampires--Fiction. 2. Dating (Social customs)--Fiction. 3.
Schools--Fiction. 4. Family life--California--Fiction. 5.
California--Fiction.] I. Title.
  PZ7.P278385Suc 2008
  [Fic]--dc22

                                                                    2007041712

U.S., CANADA,   EUROPEAN HEADQUARTERS
ASIA, PACIFIC & LATIN AMERICA   Hasbro UK Ltd
Wizards of the Coast LLC   Caswell Way
P.O. Box 707   Newport, Gwent NP9 0YH
Renton, WA 98057-0707   GREAT BRITAIN
+1-800-324-6496   Save this address for your records.

Visit our web site at www.mirrorstonebooks.com

QW - FF   09 10 11 12 13 14 15

To my husband Tony,
for everything,
and my niece Rachael,
for being my first reader.

And also to Terry,
for opening a door,
and to my editor Nina,
for being on the other side.

MYTH: Vampires don't exist.

TRUTH: Dead wrong.

1

My parents are trying to ruin my life. Oh yeah, I know that every teenager says that, but I really mean it. They want me dead. Or, actually, undead.

My parents are vampires. Some people might think that sounds cool, but I'm not talking about those romanticized bloodsuckers, like in novels where everybody walks around in ruffled white shirts and can quote poetry. I don't know where people get that stuff. Nothing could be further from the truth. My dad couldn't quote a nursery rhyme if somebody paid him. He likes to watch football and CNN. He wouldn't know (or care) who Stephenie Meyer was if she came up and bit him.

As far as I can tell being a vampire is pretty boring. Both my parents have regular jobs and have to pay bills and things like that. They don't kill people or kidnap frail young maidens to be their slaves. (At least I'm pretty sure they don't. I think I'd have noticed if there were a bunch of corpses piled up in the basement.)

Sure, they get to live for pretty much forever, but there are a lot of bad things that go along with being a vampire. Like never going to the beach again without gobs of SPF-a-million and some seriously dark sunglasses because your skin'll burn like there's no tomorrow and your super-duper eyes can't take the glare. And there's always the pressure of trying not to let the neighbors in on our little family secret.

I'm so used to it, though. I guess I'd never thought about becoming a vampire much personally. That is, until this morning. As if I didn't have enough to worry about with that huge Chemistry test today.

"Mina," Mom says, "We need to talk."

If you're wondering, yeah, they named me after that girl in Bram Stoker's *Dracula*. How cheesy can you get? I mean, hello? Obvious, anyone?

"Can it wait until after school?" I mumble around my toast. Every time she starts off that way I know it's going to be a long conversation.

"No," says Dad and actually puts the paper down.

Uh-oh. Another sign of serious trouble. I'm going over in my head everything I might have possibly done wrong, but I can't think of anything I've done lately, other than leaving my midnight snack dishes in the sink overnight.

"We need to talk to you about your future," says Mom, at the exact same time that Dad says, "You have a big decision to make."

I have absolutely no response for that, so I just stare at them. I mean, what do you say to that? Oh, goodie?

Mom smiles nervously at me and pats me on the hand like she used to do when I was a little girl. "We've been putting this off for a long time—maybe too long—but the time has come for you to choose."

"Choose what?"

Dad takes over. "Whether you want to be a vampire or not."

Wuzzah? I almost choke on my toast. "I have to decide if I want to be a vampire? Why?" I'm giving them my best stare down, which usually makes Mom cave, but not today. She looks kind of sad, but just nods.

"We probably should have said something sooner, but we thought we could get them to extend the deadline until after college at least."

"Them? Who them?" My grammar is horrible, but I don't care. This is no time to worry about stuff like that.

"The Council," explains Dad. "The Northwest Regional Vampire Council."

I must have looked really blank because Mom starts apologizing again. "I'm really sorry, honey. We really should have been telling you about this stuff all along. We just wanted you to have as normal a childhood as possible."

Excuse me? I can't even begin to go over all of the things that weren't normal about my childhood, but I don't want to get into that now. That's the kind of stuff you go to years of therapy for—which I would never do. Any therapist would probably lock you up as soon as you started explaining that your parents are vampires.

"The Council has decreed that you must make a decision."

"What's The Council got to do with it?"

"Well," he says uncomfortably, "you're in kind of a unique situation. Non-vampires aren't really supposed to know about us."

"Yeah, yeah, I know, the whole stake-through-the-heart thing. But I've known for years. Why does it make any difference now?"

Mom and Dad look at each other and then back at me. I know that look. They don't know what to say. I've got them on this one. Ha! I swoop in for the kill.

"If I was going to tell someone, I'd have done it years ago. Besides, who would believe me? The Council can't deny that." Council-shmouncil. I smile in triumph and take another bite of toast.

"It's not that easy," says Mom. "It's not the fact that you know about us that's forcing this. It's because The Council didn't know about *you*."

"So, how did they find out? I know I didn't tell them." Seeing as how no one around here ever clues me into *anything*.

They exchange another guilty look and Dad picks up the ball. "Do you remember that guy that showed up about a month ago with some papers for me?"

I did remember. I'd answered the door. He was a total freak—bald head, red-rimmed eyes, and bell-bottom pants. I hadn't pegged him for a vampire, though. I just thought he was some retro weirdo that Dad worked with. I mean, accountants are a pretty strange bunch anyway. I think it's all that staring at numbers all day.

"Well, he was from the Vampire Tax Authority. And he reported us for having a non-vampire in the household and now . . . well, now I'm afraid you're going to have to decide whether or not you want to become a vampire."

I can't believe they're letting some stupid vampire paper-pushers dictate my life. But I've still got one last dig before I give it up. I go for guilt.

"Why are you guys laying this on me right before I have to go to school? Why couldn't this have waited until later?"

Mom directs a sharp look Dad's way, and Dad ducks back behind his newspaper. She pulls it back down. Can you tell who has the fangs in my family?

"Um, well, someone might be here, um, visiting when you get back from school today. And you might not want to mention how long you've known we're vampires . . . " He hides behind the paper again.

Lucky for him, Serena picks that minute to honk her car horn outside. I grab my stuff and leave without giving them the satisfaction of a look back.

"Wassup!" Serena yells at me as I climb into her beat-up Volkswagen Beetle. She's my best friend, even if she does use ancient catchphrases all the time.

"Nothing."

She pulls out into the road, nearly running over Mrs. Finch's stupid cat, and makes a big frowny face at me. That usually will crack me up. See, Serena got into the whole Goth thing about two years ago and let me tell you, there's nothing funnier than when someone all done up in black lipstick and that thick white makeup starts making clown faces. I don't know how she can take all that stuff seriously, but I've already lived through everything from her ballerina phase to her pop-rock phase, so I figure I can get through this one. The Christina Aguilera phase (thankfully it was the pre-slut look) was the worst one so far.

"Hmmmm, methinks we have a dour one today. You want to talk about it?"

I try and smile at her, but it doesn't come out very well. "Maybe later, okay?"

I'm a miserable liar, especially with Serena. Better not to talk about things than to say something I'll regret later. We've been friends since kindergarten, but there are a few things I just can't talk to her about. Like my parents being vampires, for one. Or the fact that I have to decide whether to become one myself.

The thing is I know the answer. I don't want to be one. Sure, back when I was ten or so I had a brief cape fascination. That was right after the first time Mom showed me that she could walk on the ceiling, so I had an excuse. I mean, how cool is that? But if I thought about turning at all, it was at some point way in the future. I've got my whole life ahead of me right now. Shoot, I've still got my senior year of high school ahead of me.

Serena takes the hint and starts singing some really old Britney song at the top of her lungs. It's no wonder the other Goth chicks at school won't hang out with her.

I thought I was doing pretty well putting the whole life-changing-vampire decision out of my mind, until I got to sixth period English.

Ms. Tweeter—and no, I am not kidding you, that is her actual name—is dressed all in black and has a long red cape on. That's not as unusual as it sounds. She likes to dress up to go along with her lesson plans to "get us more involved." I don't know that it actually works at getting us more involved, but it certainly is entertaining. When we did *Hamlet*, she left a skull sitting on her desk the whole time and kept talking to it and calling it Yorick. She's kind of weird, but I usually like her. Until today.

"Class," she says in deep, sepulchral tones, "today we start a new unit on . . . *Dracula*!!!" She swirls the cape and darts around the room like a mad woman while all the jocks in the back crack up like crazy. They just *love* Ms. Tweeter.

Man, out of all the books we could be studying, she has to pick this one. Probably the main source of vampire misinformation out there. Not that I've read it. But I've seen some of the movies and they suck. Pun intended.

I sink a little lower in my seat. Serena, sitting next to me, is clapping her hands like a good little Goth girl.

Ms. Tweeter settles down a little and returns to the front of the classroom. "*Dracula* was published in 1897 by Bram Stoker. While not a best seller in its time, it became popular in the 1920s and 30s when various portrayals of the evil Count hit the silver screen. Maybe you've heard of Bela Lugosi?"

She looks around the room as a few of us nod our heads. My crazy uncle Mortie dresses up like Lugosi every year at Halloween. You'd think The Council would be all over that, but no-o-o-o.

"Many believe that the character Dracula is based on Vlad the Impaler—" Tim Mathis, in the second row, starts thrashing around in his chair and making dying noises, but Ms. Tweeter just continues on like nothing is happening—"but there's little evidence that Mr. Stoker researched Vlad or knew much about him. In fact, the original name of the character was to be Count Wampyr." Ms. Tweeter hands Tim a stack of papers and makes motions for him to pass them out to the class as she keeps talking. Payback for acting like an idiot. "Now, I'm sure all of you have heard of vampires and have pre-conceived notions of what vampires are like. Anyone have any examples?"

I sink even lower into the chair. I am definitely not taking the bait on this one. Serena raises her hand and so do a couple of other kids.

9

"They can't go out in sunlight," says Serena.

"You can get rid of them with garlic or holy water," says Bethany Madison, the total suck up.

"Or stakes!" This from Tim, still passing out the handouts.

"Good, good," says Ms. Tweeter. "All common conceptions, but somewhat wrong. You'll be surprised to find that Count Dracula *can* go out in sunlight and that his ultimate demise is not the result of a stake through the heart." I sit up a little, but not enough to tempt Ms. Tweeter to call on me. I know darn well vampires can go out in the sunlight, but I didn't realize that the book got that right.

"The handout you're getting has your reading schedule for the next four weeks and some assignment choices. Tonight's homework assignment is for everyone. Before reading the book, write down all the vampire myths you know of. We'll be doing a comparison at the end to see how what you think you know stacks up against the book. And, you'll need to pick one main project to work on by the end of the week to turn in at the end of the unit. I've included some reading prompts and a character listing to help you out."

She looks right at me then. Oh man, I silently plead with her, don't do it, but, of course, she does. "And we've got the perfect Mina right here with us for our class readings!" Everyone turns to look at me. Thanks a lot, Ms. Tweeter. I really needed that pointed out.

After class, I take my time getting out of there. I'm not in any rush to get home to find out who our mystery visitor might be. Serena is so excited she's chatting my ear off about the whole *Dracula* thing. I love her like a sister, but sometimes, she's a total geekoid.

"Hey, Mina," yells Tim, "You vant to suck my blood?"

My heart totally stops—How does he know? Then I realize he's just being Tim. Now, normally, I'd totally blow him off because he's a flaming idiot, but today it just so happens that Nathan is right on his heels.

Nathan Able. As in Nathan I'm-Able-to-Rock-Your-World. Nathan Very-Kiss-Able. Nathan, the cutest guy in the entire school—no, the entire town and maybe even the entire state of California. Nathan, the guy I've been crushing on since like the sixth grade. So instead of putting Tim in his place like I generally would (and he deserves), I stand there like a total loser with my mouth hanging open until Serena comes to the rescue.

"Mina doesn't even become a vampire in the book," she says loftily. "Maybe you should do some actual *reading* this year, Tim." She pulls me down the hall and out the door. I do my best not to look back in Nathan's direction, especially since I think my mouth is still hanging open.

"Thanks," I say.

"No problem. I know how you are about *Nathan*. I wouldn't mind munching on his neck myself." She bares her teeth at me in a pretty decent movie-vampire imitation and I can't help but laugh. Boy, what she doesn't know . . .

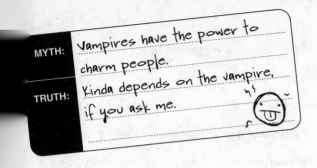

MYTH: Vampires have the power to charm people.

TRUTH: Kinda depends on the vampire, if you ask me.

2

Before Serena even drops me off after school, I know who at least one of our "special" visitors is. Uncle Mortie's huge old Cadillac is out front, taking up like half the block, with a plain white Toyota right behind it.

"Looks like your uncle Mortie's here. Message me later?"

"Sure," I mumble and climb out of her car. I wave at her and wait until she's gone before turning to face the house. I just stand and stare at it, trying to get my feet to go in there to face the music. Or the fangs. Whatever.

Uncle Mortie is actually Great-Uncle Mortie and he's the real reason we're in this mess. He was the first one in the family to turn. He's also more or less a total flake. See, he's a traveling salesman and before you say it, yeah, they really do still have those. He sells vacuums or something like that door-to-door. Not

13

that I can imagine him selling too many. I know I wouldn't open the door if I saw him on the other side.

From what I've overheard over the years (and let me tell you, eavesdropping isn't easy when your parents can hear a bee a mile away), he was turned around the time I was conceived. Somewhere in the middle of Kansas he knocked on this likely looking door. Some blond lady invited him in, and I guess she was wearing some cute little outfit that got his blood all a-boiling so much that he doesn't even notice she's got fangs and more than a passing interest in his neck. (Which I kind of understand, since Uncle Mortie is a *complete* sucker for blondes. He once went through three rolls of quarters at the state fair so he could chat up this blond girl running one of the booths while I pitched darts at balloons. I didn't even win anything.)

I'm not sure what happened to the blond bombshell, but, next thing you know, he's a fiftysome-year-old balding vampire with a pot belly. So then he winds up biting my dad and infecting him during some kind of argument, even though Dad's his favorite nephew. Or is that great-nephew? Whatever. Mom followed along on purpose a few months later, after she had me. She loved Dad too much to leave him over something like a little bloodsucking. And that was that, I guess.

I take a deep breath and go in the front door. Uncle Mortie

is lounging on the couch next to an old lady in a flowery dress with her hair all done up in a bun. Mom and Dad are nowhere to be seen.

"How's my favorite niece?" booms Uncle Mortie.

"Your only niece." I shoot back before I remember to mind my manners in front of the stranger.

Uncle Mortie just laughs it off. "See, I told you she was a spitfire!" he says to the lady sitting next to him. I assume she's a vampire. But she's a very unlikely looking one.

Actually, I take that back. Every vampire I know is an unlikely looking one. Uncle Mortie *looks* like a traveling salesman.

The lady is kind of short and dumpy and very friendly looking. I can picture her with lots of grandkids, baking chocolate chip cookies, things like that.

"Hello, Mina," says the lady in this very sweet voice, reinforcing the whole grandmotherly image she has going on. She picks some invisible fuzz off of her old-fashioned dress and smiles at me very sincerely. I don't really want to like her, but it's hard not to smile back. I can practically smell the cookies. She pats a spot on the couch right next to her for me to sit down.

"Mina, meet Josephine Riley. She's . . ."

"I'm the Northwest Regional Vampire Council's new member indoctrinator." She smiles again. "I'm in charge of introducing

15

teens like you to the vampire culture and helping you make a responsible decision regarding whether to make the transition from human life to vampire life."

Before I can stop myself, I blurt out, "That sounds like it's straight out of a brochure: Vampirism and You."

Uncle Mortie shoots me a nasty look this time but Ms. Riley just smiles. "Actually, it is."—she pulls a pamphlet out of her bag and holds it out to me—"Though it's called 'The Vampire Way.' I wrote it myself."

I grab the pamphlet before Uncle Mortie says anything. I really do have to learn to keep my mouth shut.

"I just wanted to introduce myself as your coordinator and give you the opportunity to ask any questions you might have. I know this must be a really difficult time for you. Finding out your parents are vampires must have been a huge shock."

Uncle Mortie is practically having a spasm nodding at me, so I go along with it. Though, seriously, does this Riley lady think I'm a total idiot? How do you *not* notice your parents are bloodsucking vampires? I mean, we live in the same house. I know some teenagers are oblivious, but *please*.

"Yeah, I could hardly believe it." I hear myself saying. "And Uncle Mortie too! I always knew something was wrong with him, I just didn't know what." I smile sweetly at Uncle Mortie.

Uncle Mortie grimaces at me (I'm sure I'll hear about that later), and Riley makes some sympathetic noises.

I thumb through the pamphlet. I have no desire to be some bloodsucking freak, but I can't deny that I've been curious about how it all works. Mom and Dad don't really talk about specifics too much and Uncle Mortie . . . Well, let's just say that my parents don't like him to talk about anything important in front of me. He tends to let slip some of the more, shall we say, *interesting* details.

"Mortimer has kindly agreed to be your sponsor. He'll be your guide during this decision-making period." It takes me a minute to figure out that Mortimer must be Uncle Mortie.

"Yep, kiddo," he says with a wicked gleam in his eye that doesn't bode well for my Dad's blood pressure (that is, if he had any). "You can ask me anything."

I almost laugh out loud. I can't believe my parents agreed to this. Then Ms. Riley drops the other shoe on me.

"And you'll have to attend my information sessions of course. I'm running a short five-week introductory course that I've taken the liberty of signing you up for. You've already missed the first week, I'm afraid." She looks a little miffed at that. "I'd put you in the next course starting up, but that one is for adults only. Given your unique situation and the recommendation of The Council, I thought it best to get you started in the classes right away."

"I have to attend classes? Like vampire lessons or something?"

"Oh yes," she says, getting up and taking my hand in a firm grip. She looks deep in my eyes. "I'm sure you'll find them very enlightening."

I've got a smart comment right on the tip of my tongue, but there's something about her gaze that holds me there like a trapped animal. She may look like a grandmother and sound like one, but there's something much harder underneath. Like the wolf in grandma's dress from that old fairy tale. It feels like her eyes are boring right through my skull. Am I not acting shocked enough? Can she tell how long I've known about my parents?

Uncle Mortie clears his throat and stands up too. That's enough to tear my gaze away from Grandma Wolfington and gather my scattered brains back together. She is one wickedly weird woman.

"How many sessions are there?" I ask in what I hope is a polite tone. I turn my eyes back to the pamphlet and flip through it some more. I don't want to get stuck in Grandma Wolfington's gaze again. Who knows what she can see with those freaky eyes.

"Two sessions a week—Tuesdays and Thursdays—for the next four weeks. It's unfortunate that you've missed two already, but your *uncle Mortimer* assures me that he can cover some aspects of your training." Grandma Wolfington doesn't even glance in Uncle Mortie's direction when she says his name. I'm starting to get the feeling that she doesn't like him very much. Maybe he brings out the worst in her, just like he does in me. (Oh man, the time he got me that water gun for my fourth birthday and taught me how to aim low. Everyone walked around for a week looking like they'd peed their pants until Dad got the gun away from me.)

"We'll get started with your training tonight." Uncle Mortie puts in. "I'm staying for dinner. I understand your mom's making fried chicken and mashed potatoes." He rubs his hands together and practically jumps up and down in glee. I catch Wolfington rolling her eyes at him, but she smiles politely enough, shakes my hand one more time, and takes her leave with just one more parting shot.

"I'll see you tomorrow, Mina. Don't be late. And don't forget to fill out and bring Form 1063-A with you. I left a copy with your uncle." She holds the door ajar and turns back to pierce me with another look. "And Mina? We'll be watching you." With that, she leaves.

I gotta say, the lady knows how to make a dramatic exit.

MYTH: Vampires don't eat

TRUTH: Uh, have you ever met my uncle Mortie?

3

Here's lesson one, Mina my dear," says Uncle Mortie around a mouthful of fried chicken. I swear he has an entire drumstick shoved in there. He's not exactly long on couth, if you know what I mean. "Vampires don't *have* to eat. Well, other than blood that is." I can't quite keep myself from cringing a little. I mean, we're at the dinner table and the first thing he wants to talk about is blood? "But we *can* eat. And when the cooking is as good as your mother's, why wouldn't we?" He lets out a hearty laugh and a little bit of chicken sprays out of his mouth and lands on the tablecloth.

"Duh, Uncle Mortie." Sheesh. Not like I haven't been living with my parents all this time or anything.

Mom gives me a be-polite glare and then stares a little pointedly at the piece of chicken lying on the table. Dad notices and very quietly picks it up with his napkin. Uncle Mortie, of course, just keeps on eating. Mom's not a huge fan of Uncle Mortie or his table manners. I really can't believe that they agreed to let him sponsor me. In fact, why did they?

"So how come Uncle Mortie's my sponsor and not you guys?" I ask Mom.

She looks a little pained. "The Council isn't exactly happy with us. And they thought your father and I might be a little too close to the situation to be objective."

"Yeah," Uncle Mortie chimes in, "I'm both objective and objectionable." He's still chewing on the chicken like there's no tomorrow.

Mom just ignores him. "This is a big decision, honey, and we want you to make the right choice for you. Don't let our feelings get in the way of things."

Well, hello, like they even could. It is my life, after all. Not that they've exactly said what their thoughts on the subject are. Do they actually want their only daughter to be a bloodsucking vampire or what? "So, what do you feel about it?" I look back and forth from Mom to Dad. Neither one of them says a word. They don't even look at each other, so it's obvious that they worked this out ahead of time. Dad doesn't have that great of a poker face normally. Perfect. "You can't even give me a clue?"

"Afraid not," says Dad. "That's just not the way it works. It really needs to be your decision."

"With only Uncle Mortie to help me decide?"

Are they kidding me? I might get the scoop on the best places to pick up blond vampire chicks from him or where you can buy the best rare burger in town, but I don't know that I want to have the biggest decision of my life hinge on stuff like that.

"Hey," says Uncle Mortie, looking a little hurt. He uses his napkin to wipe some bits of mashed potato off his face. "I promise I'll be good," he says. "I know this is a big decision for you, kiddo."

"Yeah, okay," I say. But I can't help but notice the worried look on Mom's face. I can't tell though . . . is she worried that Uncle Mortie will talk me out of it or into it?

"But what's the deal with these classes anyway? For vampires trying to keep it on the down-low, they sure do seem to be awfully public about it."

Uncle Mortie and Dad get twin sour looks on their face. Uncle Mortie mutters something about "blasted paper-pushing" something-or-others. Mom passes him some biscuits.

"Why can't you guys just tell me everything I need to know? I mean, you *are* vampires. What are they going to tell me that you couldn't?"

"Mina, please just try and keep an open mind." Dad sighs. "The Council has put this process in place and everyone has to go through it. They . . . we . . . we really need you to just get through this, okay?" He looks to Mom for some backup.

"They just want to make sure that anyone turning nowadays knows what they are getting into. They believe that a formal class setting helps get the information across," she says diplomatically.

Yeah. I bet. I'm sure that's why. That probably came right out of one of Wolfington's brochures.

"And it's just a month. That's not too long, right? Then it will all be over."

Maybe Dad was trying to make me feel better but it also makes me put two and two together. "Does that mean I have to actually make my decision in a month? In just four weeks?"

Dad looks at Mom again. He's definitely not batting a thousand today. "Yes, I'm afraid so. But I'm sure the sessions will—"

"Fine." I interrupt and get up from the dinner table. I normally wouldn't be so rude, but this isn't exactly a normal situation. "Fine. I'll go to the stupid vampire classes for you guys. And make my decision or whatever."

But I don't tell them what I'm really thinking. I'll sit through the stupid classes or whatever The Council pushes on me, but I've got no plans to sprout fangs anytime soon. What's the point?

I skip dessert and go up to my room. I'm sure Uncle Mortie will have no problem eating my share anyway.

WHY IT SUCKS TO BE ME

1. I have freaks for parents. Sure, yeah, every teenager thinks their parents are freaks. I know mine are. Bloodsucking freaks. Not that they're bad freaks, but still.

2. As if high school wasn't bad enough, now I have to go to vampire classes with a bunch of weirdos who actually want to suck blood.

3. The vampire classes are taught by some crazy grandmother-with-fangs.

4. And I bet we'll have some lame homework in these classes too. Like practicing our bloodsucking techniques on fruit or, you know, essays on why being a vampire would make us a better person (yeah, right), or writing profiles of famous vampires in history. Bo-ring.

5. My degenerate uncle Mortie is supposed to help guide me in all this? I don't think so.

6. Then there's my complete inability to talk in complete sentences around cute boys. (Especially Nathan. He probably thinks I've got a speech impediment or something. And what if they make us do something stupid in those vampire classes, like wear practice fangs or something? I'll never be able to open my mouth in public again!)

7. And I can't tell Serena, the one person who really understands me, about any of this. Well, she already knows about the boy issues (it's obvious), but I could really use someone to talk to about the whole vampire thing.

8. But the absolute worst thing is that it's so totally unfair that I have to make one of the biggest decisions of my life when I'm only sixteen (almost seventeen, but still). They don't even let you vote until you're eighteen!

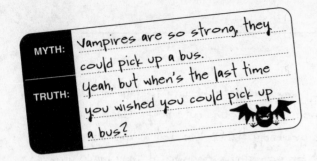

MYTH: Vampires are so strong, they could pick up a bus.

TRUTH: Yeah, but when's the last time you wished you could pick up a bus?

4

Okay, in case you hadn't gathered this already, vampires, in general, look absolutely nothing like Brad Pitt or Tom Cruise or David Boreanaz or any actor at all, for that matter. Which is why I am not at all surprised to walk into my first vampire lesson and see a couple of Average Joe kids wandering around reading the posters on the rec room walls.

I'm starting to think The Council must be short on funds or something. Couldn't they have found someplace a little better than a local community center? Maybe somewhere with just a little bit of atmosphere and a little less B.O.? The sign on the door actually says Teen Phlebotomy Group. I mean, you've got to be kidding me. Someone has a strange sense of humor.

I'm here early because . . .

a) Dad drove me and he's really anal (that accountant thing), besides being a horrible driver,

b) I had to get out of the house before Mom started snapping pictures like I was going to the prom or something, and

c) I totally hate to be the last one walking into a room full of strangers. I'd much rather be the person safely gawking at the new guy from somewhere in the back of the room than the sucker who walks in last. First isn't really good either, since then you're stuck there waiting until other people come in, but third or fourth is perfect. It's bad enough I'm the new girl, which means everyone will be staring at me anyway.

I've timed it about right since there are two girls and one guy in the room already. I don't recognize any of them from my school, which I guess is a good thing. One of the girls is on the Goth side (figures there'd be at least one), but the other one could pass for, you know, a girl from the chess club or something. The guy is just normal-looking (pretty good hair, a little taller than me, but definitely not an A-lister—he looks too friendly), another vampire-unlikely.

I saunter as casually as I can over toward the ring of chairs in the middle of the room. Great, looks like it's going to be one of those feel-goody type of classes where we have to *share*. I don't make it halfway before Ms. Chess Club scampers over to me and grabs my hand. So much for being inconspicuous.

"Hi! I'm Linda!" She's pumping my hand up and down like she's trying out for world's most annoying handshake.

"Uh, hi, Linda. I'm Mina."

She's still going for the record like there's no tomorrow with a huge grin on her face. I smile back but I can feel my hand going numb.

"Let the poor girl go, Linda," says the Goth girl. "You don't have to *kill* everyone with *kindness*." She practically spits the words out. I'm not sure which thing she thinks is the bad thing.

Linda drops my hand like it caught on fire. "Oh, I'm so sorry! I always do that!"

"It's okay," I say, totally confused. Now she looks like she's about to cry.

"I'm Raven," says Goth girl. I nod at her. Of course she is. Aren't all good Goth girls named Raven? Except Serena, but that's how I know she's just temporary-Goth. She'd never call herself something cheesy like "Raven." Because you *know* that's not her real name, not unless her parents are even freakier than mine.

"You're new." I nod again. I am amazed at the mystical powers of Raven the Goth Girl. Okay, I know I'm laying it on a little thick, but there's something about this girl I just don't like. I don't like it when people are rude to other people for no reason. Ms. Chess Club wasn't bothering me that much, but she's wandered off to another corner of the room to read a safety poster, so I guess she's recovering okay from Ms. Goth Girl's insult.

Goth Girl stares me up and down. "Just stay away from Aubrey, and we'll be fine," she says and walks away.

I have no clue who or what an Aubrey is. But whoever or whatever Aubrey is, I am determined to not stay away from him. Or her. Or it. Agh! Bossy Goth Girls really tick me off.

I take a seat as far as I can across the circle from Goth Girl. Linda, interestingly enough, sits down right next to her. Figures. The black-hearted leading the weak. Mr. Quiet sits somewhere in between, still not having said a single word or having even looked in my direction as far as I can tell. Oh yeah, this'll be a fun group. I'm bonding already.

Ms. Riley, aka Grandma Wolfington, comes in next carrying a stack of visual aids. She nods and smiles at me and everyone else and putters around getting everything ready, exuding even more grandmotherliness. But I know better.

A few more people trickle in and take seats. A girl wearing a cheerleading outfit—a cheerleading outfit!—sits down next to me.

"Hey," she says with a big shiny smile. "You must be new! My name is Lorelai. I go to West Haven. Home of the Flying Eagles! How about you?"

I force myself to look away from her shiny white teeth. Cheerleaders aren't high up on my list usually, but she seems decent, especially compared to Goth Girl.

"Uh, I go to McAdam. And I'm Mina."

"Nice to meet you," she says, smiling even wider. What is it with wannabe-vampires and smiles a mile wide anyway? A mouth fixation or something?

"I'm so excited," Lorelai gushes. "I think we're going to talk about some of the physical changes today. You know, like what happens with your muscles and things. My body is really important to me"—I swear she flexes a bicep at me—" 'cause I cheer now and I'd really love to be a professional cheerleader once I get out of high school. Being a vampire could really help me with that."

A professional cheerleader vampire? Oh man, hold Uncle Mortie back. I've officially heard everything now.

"What about the whole drinking blood thing?" I ask. Based on my limited experience with cheerleaders, I'd guess that she'd be more of a vodka girl.

She just giggles, not exactly the reaction I was expecting. "Hey, if I can drink a protein shake, I can drink anything."

"Ah," I say since she's looking at me expectantly. "Hey, who or what is an Aubrey anyway?"

Lorelai gets a moony look on her face and sighs. "Raven must have said something to you, right?" I nod. "She's got a total crush on him. You'll just have to see for yourself why. Actually . . . here he comes now."

I turn halfway around to see whoever's coming through the door, in order to be as inconspicuous as I can. No need to let Goth Girl know what I'm up to yet.

Oh.

My.

God.

Okay, you know what I said about vampires not looking like Brad Pitt or Tom Cruise or those actors on *Buffy*? It's obvious I was really, really wrong because walking through the door is the most gorgeous hunk of man-flesh I have ever seen (well, besides Nathan). And he even looks like the stereotypical movie vampire guy—tall, thin, longish brown hair that perfectly frames his face. Intense green eyes. I can feel myself blush as he glances in my direction. I turn around quickly.

"That's Aubrey," says Lorelai, a little unnecessarily.

"Wow."

"Yeah, I know." She turns and stares at him openly. "If I

didn't already have a great boyfriend, I would totally go fo him."

Oh, man. Even if I *had* a boyfriend, I would still totally go fo him. I sneak another peek. He's chatting with Grandma Wolfing ton and showing her some book he brought with him. From what I can see of the cover, it looks like your typical vampire romance fiction (tall Fabio-like dude in a cloak with his arms wrapped around some long-haired girl about to swoon). He's got questionable reading habits, but everything else looks great. Perfect long fingers. Clean nails. Lovely hands.

He doesn't strike me as the Goth type, even though he's got a little bit of a Renaissance thing going on with the outfit he's got on. On anyone else, it would look really stupid. I wonder if Ms. Goth Girl actually has a claim on him or if it's all wishful thinking.

"Well, looks like everyone is here," says Grandma Wolfington. Aubrey takes a seat along with all the rest of the stragglers. I note with some glee that he doesn't sit next to Raven, even though she's saved him a seat and looks like she's about to have an apoplectic fit trying to wave him into it.

"As you've probably noticed, we've got someone new today. Why don't you stand up and introduce yourself," says Grandma Wolfington, looking at me.

So I stand up and go "Hey, I'm Mina." They all just stare at me blankly. "You know, like from *Dracula*?" I can't believe I said that. To *these* people in particular. I give myself a mental whack in the head.

Grandma Wolfington nods brightly as if I hadn't said anything stupid and motions for me to sit down. "Mina's parents are vampires, though she only recently found out she's been living with vampires her whole life."

That gets a rise out of the group, and they all look at me with interest for the first time, especially Aubrey, the sexy vampire wannabe.

"I'm sure you will all welcome Mina into the group." She treats everyone to a moment of her patented glare and they all nod like good little vampire trainees.

"Today we're going to be discussing the changes in musculature and physical appearance that occur when you turn." Grandma Wolfington points to a chart of the human body hanging on the wall. "The first changes affect the lean muscle mass in your body . . . "

Half an hour later and my eyes are completely starting to glaze over. This is worse than chemistry! Who knew there was so much science involved in turning. And honestly, I really didn't care. It all boiled down to:

a) you get stronger,

b) you don't get tired or have to sleep anymore (which I totally already knew—sneaking out of my house is so not an option), and

c) you should never let a human doctor get a gander at your insides or else you'll be locked away in some top-secret facility and no one will ever see you again.

But everyone else was following Grandma Wolfington's every word like their lives depended on it. I wouldn't be surprised if G.W. started passing around Kool-Aid.

"And you know what else is awesome?" Lorelai leans in and whispers to me when Grandma Wolfington pauses for a minute. "We'll never gain any weight! Ever! Not to be mean, but if I were Linda, I'd go ahead and knock off those extra ten pounds now, if you know what I mean." She glances thoughtfully in Ms. Chess Club's direction. "You think I should mention that to her?"

I shake my head and stifle a yawn behind my hand. I can't imagine it would do any good to point out to someone that they need to lose weight. Like she doesn't already know. She *is* a girl. "How long does this go on?" I whisper back.

"Oh, only about a half hour longer," she sighs. "There's just so much to learn! I don't know how we'll ever get through it all with these short sessions!"

I successfully smother a snort, which is no easy task, let me tell you.

"You're so lucky," Lorelai whispers. "All of this must be old news to you."

I just shrug as noncommittally as possible. She's *probably* not a spy for Grandma Wolfington, but who knows. Though it's not like I really do know any of this stuff. It's not exactly the kind of thing that we sit around the dinner table and talk about. But who would? Muscle mass, fast-twitch muscles, blah, blah, blah. I just hope there's not a quiz.

I make it through the rest of the lecture, but just barely. G.W. is definitely pro-vampire. So much for "helping me make my decision" and all that feel-good talk about how it's my choice. She goes on and on about all the good stuff that happens, but never covers any of the bad stuff, like:

a) Not being able to tell your friends anything, though they are bound to wonder why you suddenly like your steak raw. *Really* raw.

b) Drinking blood. I'm sorry, it's just gross. *Way* worse than sushi.

c) The massive headaches you get if you happen to forget your sunglasses (just ask my dad, who barely remembers his shoes on a good day).

35

d) Not being able to sleep. At all. Forgive me, but I like my pillow time. And what about dreams? I can skip the nightmares, but a good dream about Nathan can hold me for a week.

e) Having to constantly control your bloodlust when you're around regular people. Though even thinking about the word "lust" and my parents in the same thought is totally lunch-losing.

f) Unintentionally hurting the people you love. Like the time Mom accidentally broke my finger when I was ten—she was just tossing a Frisbee with me. I think she felt worse than I did (though I have to admit that I milked that for as much ice cream as I could).

g) Always being suspicious and afraid that people have found out your little vampire secret. Like our nosy neighbor, Mrs. Finch. She'd have a telescope pointed at our window if she thought she could get away with it.

But it's not like I can say anything, so I tune out the really over–the-top stuff and spend the other half of my time (okay, maybe more than half) staring dreamily at Aubrey.

I stand up and grab my stuff, all ready to jet out of the vampire propaganda session when Aubrey himself (!) actually walks right up to me.

"Hello, new girl," he says in this oh-holy-moly deep voice. I concentrate on not dropping anything or doing something really dorky, like drooling all over him.

"Nice to meet you," I say. "Aubrey, right?" Oops, I probably shouldn't have let on that I knew his name. Smooth, I'm not.

"Yes, that's me." He smiles and I nearly faint right there on the spot. Oh, wow, if Serena could just get a look at this guy. She would totally flip. "I need to get home tonight, but I was wondering if you'd like to catch a cup of coffee or something after school tomorrow. I'd love to ask you some questions."

Yes! Score one for Mina! "Um, sure," I say. "How about the Coffee Café on Tower Road?" I'm totally melting inside, but I am very proud of how well I seem to be holding it together. Except for the bead of sweat I suddenly feel coursing down my back, but at least he can't see that.

"Sounds great." He smiles again. "I'll see you then."

He takes off and I stare after him, letting out a breath that I didn't even realize I was holding. Lorelai slaps me a high five.

"You go, girl!" she says. She scribbles a number on a piece of paper and hands it to me. "And I want to hear all about it. You give me a call tomorrow night, okay?"

"Will do," I say. I cannot believe my luck. Maybe this whole vampire lesson thing is a blessing in disguise and not just

something to get through to keep my parents happy and The
Council off our backs. Maybe this is the starting point for a
whole new Mina. Not necessarily in a whole new bloodsucking
kind of-way, but at least on the boy front. I've got no history with
Aubrey and if I can just hold it together and not flake out, maybe
I can give Goth Girl something to worry about.

I can feel Raven's eyes burrowing a hole in my head, so I take
off. But I don't wipe the smile off my face. She might as well get
used to it.

MYTH: Vampires can speak all languages.

TRUTH: Boy, do I wish that was true.

5

I wake up still incredibly psyched about Aubrey. I can't wait to tell Serena because she will totally and completely flip when she sees this guy. But wait . . . What am I supposed to do? Tell her I met the guy at vampire camp? I'm still puzzling over how I can tell her without letting the cat out of the bag when I get in her car to go to school. Luckily, she takes it out of my hands as soon as I'm settled in the Death Beetle. (Her car is a rusty, black original V.W. Beetle, circa her dad's college years. What else would you call it?)

"Can't talk today," Serena says. "Conjugating!"

Serena has been taking Latin since the ninth grade. I have no idea why. In my opinion, dead languages should just stay dead. I mean, they're dead for a reason, right? I, on the other hand, have been taking the language of love, French. That's not to say that I can actually speak French or carry on a conversation with a hot guy (in French or English). I can't.

"*Amo, amare, amavi, amatum*," says Serena.

I discovered the secret to getting by in French during my first year with Madame Tilly. French essentially sounds like gargling or a babbling brook, if you're being kind. So if you pronounce a word or two and just garble the rest, you can fool almost anyone. You just have to act like you know what you're saying. Madame Tilly'd like us to think she was born and raised in Paris, but she's no more French than a French fry. I'm her star pupil.

"*Navigo, navigare, navigavi, navigatum.*"

But poor Serena sticks to her Latin. I think her dad makes her take it because he wants her to go to med school some day. Or maybe he just wants to torture her. I guess I'm lucky. My parents never do anything like that. They just make me choose whether I want to be human or not. Hello!

"*Facio, facere, feci . . .*"

"*Fee-cee?* Did you just say what I think you said?"

"Shhh! Conjugating!"

I still have no idea whether my parents want me to do it or not. Turn, that is. Dad didn't say a word when he picked me up last night. Granted, I wasn't really thinking about anything but that dreamy Aubrey. Dad could have been spouting the Declaration of Independence and I wouldn't have known it.

"Maneo, manere, mansi, mansum."

I need to sit down and have a heart-to-heart with Mom. I can usually wheedle something out of her if I ask in the right way. It doesn't work as well as when I was six and unbelievably cute (seriously, I have the photos), but I've still got it.

"Scribo, scribere, scripsi, scriptum."

"You ever notice that all those verbs basically sound like 'rectum'?"

Serena just shoots me a keep-quiet-I-know-where-you-live look and keeps conjugating. I shut up for the rest of the ride.

Lunch rolls around and I still haven't figured out how I am going to tell her about Aubrey. And tell her I must! You can't keep a guy like that a secret and I had a date—a date!—with him right after school. Okay, a coffee-date, but that totally counts in my world.

Latin was her first period class so I couldn't hide behind her conjugations anymore. I grab our usual table and a plate of fries. (Okay, yeah, I know—not the healthiest meal on the planet, but have you ever tried the meatloaf surprise? There's a surprise all right. And it usually hits you around about fifth period.)

Serena finally comes in and sits down across from me. "Fries again?" she asks as she unpacks her own healthy soy-something-or-other.

I'm right about to launch into a convoluted story about how I met this guy while at the mall, ignoring the fact that my story is totally unbelievable since it would mean that I went shopping without her, which I never do. Not that I was. Whatever.

But then, suddenly, Mr. Quiet from last night just appears right behind Serena. I almost choke on a soggy fry.

"Hi, Mina," he says. "It's George. From last night?"

"Last night?" says Serena with a lifted eyebrow.

He barely even glances at Serena. "Yeah, at the . . . "

"The thing, uh, that my parents made me go to. I told you, didn't I?" Serena looks at me skeptically, but at least George gets the hint and shuts his mouth. Hello, vampire-boy, don't you remember the "Don't Tell" policy? Do I have to do all The Council's work for them? "At the museum. The new lecture series? About, uh . . . "

"The mating habits of orangutans," says George with a smirk.

I give him a really dirty look as Serena's eyebrow climbs even higher. "Um, yeah, it was really *educational*."

Serena's eyebrow goes back down a notch and I breathe a sigh of relief. *The mating habits of orangutans*. What was he thinking? I can't believe she bought that.

"So, George. I didn't know you went to McAdam too. You didn't mention that last night." In fact, I don't think he said a word through the entire vampire lesson.

"We had homeroom together last year," he says in this sad, serious voice.

"Oh." Oh man. I'm not sure what to say. How terrible am I? I completely don't remember him at all. Am I as bad as Bethany and all her friends? Do I walk all over people without realizing it? Or is he just *that* unmemorable? I mean, he is seriously normal-looking. There's nothing wrong with him or anything, but he kind of blends, you know?

The silence is kind of stretching on, so I add, "Sorry."

He laughs. "I'm just kidding," he says. "I just transferred here a couple of months ago."

Serena cracks up. "He totally had you going!"

"Did not." Ugh, I can't believe he got me like that.

"Did too!"

"So, anyway, George, what's up?" I put on my best ignore-the-situation-and-move-on smile.

"Well, since you missed the other *lectures*, I thought you might want to borrow my notes. In case there was anything you wanted to know that you weren't there to hear."

Serena's eyebrow goes back up into dangerous territory. "About the mating habits of monkeys?"

"Orangutans aren't monkeys," I say automatically.

"They aren't?" say George and Serena in unison.

"No," I say, "they're apes. Monkeys have tails. Apes don't." Ha! At least I've learned something from all those years watching Animal Planet. And Mom says TV's not good for anything. I can't quite keep myself from paying George back for the whole orangutan thing. "Guess you must not have been paying attention last night."

He laughs again. "Got me," he says. At least he's a good sport. "Anyway, I thought we could go over my notes after school today."

"I can't today, I have a thing."

"A thing?" he asks.

Oops. I give Serena a look of apology. She's going to kill me for not having told her first. "Yeah, I kind of have a date."

"A date?" Serena shrieks. "You didn't tell me you had a date tonight! On a Wednesday? With who? What? Where? When? Why?"

"Well, not like a date-date. It's a coffee date. We're just having coffee."

"O-KAY. Who is it you're just having coffee with then?"

I glance at George. "Another guy I met at the lecture. His name's Aubrey."

George gets a look on his face like he just swallowed an entire lemon. "Oh," he says. "Well, I'll see you in the next lecture then." He starts to walk away.

He's probably just jealous of Aubrey (I mean, who wouldn't be?), but now I feel terrible for the second time in like five minutes. "Hold on, George. Maybe we could go over your notes before tomorrow night's, um, lecture?"

"Sure," he says and gives me a crooked half-smile. "I'll meet you there half an hour early." He's actually not so bland when he smiles. He gives us a jaunty little wave as he walks off.

Serena doesn't even notice that he's gone. "So dish it, girl. What's this mystery man look like? What're his particulars?"

I sigh and draw up Aubrey in my mind like I have a thousand times already today. "Okay, hair like Brad Pitt in *Interview with a Vampire* and eyes like Tom Welling from *Smallville*, except green. A body like Christian Bale in, I dunno, anything. And kind of an Orlando Bloom-ish vibe. But more *Pirates of the Caribbean* than *Elizabethtown*."

Serena lets that sink in a minute and lets out an appreciative whistle. "Nice. And you met this guy in a lecture about the sex habits of monkeys?"

"Orangutans."

"Orangutans. Whatever." She shakes her head. "Where are these lectures at again? I might need to come check them out. Maybe all the good guys are obsessed with monkey sex or something. They sure aren't hanging around McAdam."

Uh-oh. I can't have her following me or showing up at the museum and finding out there's no lecture. "Nah, he was the only really cute guy there. And the next lecture is on like basket weaving or something like that. I don't think there'll be too many guys at that one."

"That George guy is going though, right?"

"Yeah, but I think his parents must be making him go too. You know, like we don't get enough learning in school already." I dig into my plate of cold fries hoping she'll drop the subject.

"He's kind of cute."

It takes me a few to figure out she must mean our lunchtime visitor. "George?"

"Yeah, in a bookish kind of way."

"Oh? He does have a pretty good smile."

"Well, maybe you can introduce me next time." She wags a finger at me. Yeesh, she's right. I completely forgot to do the whole polite name-exchange thing. I would totally flunk a Miss Manners class.

"Sorry!"

"S'okay. I'm sure you had your big date on your mind." She finishes her sandwich and carefully wraps up all the stray bean sprout bits and whatnot all nice and neat. Hmmm. I wonder if George is into neat-freak-faux-Goth girls?

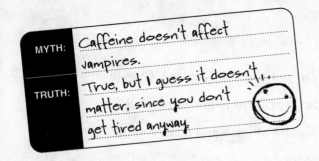

MYTH: Caffeine doesn't affect vampires.

TRUTH: True, but I guess it doesn't matter, since you don't get tired anyway.

6

I get to the Coffee Café within record time after school, making my first stop the kitschy retro bathroom after checking to make sure Aubrey wasn't there yet. I'm not the girliest of girls (I only own like five pairs of shoes and just one lipstick that I borrowed from my mom and never gave back), but I'd gotten up an entire hour earlier just to pick out my outfit. And that was after lying there and obsessing about it half the night. Considering how much I love sleep, that's really saying a lot for how hot Aubrey is.

I'm still not entirely happy with what I wound up wearing, but I figure he saw me last night in my oldest pair of jeans and a T-shirt. Anything is bound to be an improvement over that. If I'd known there was going to be a hottie in attendance, I'd have put much more effort into it. So, today I've got on this dark red shirt that my dad hates (cleavage alert!) and my best pair of butt-hugging low-rider jeans. At least I'm tall enough to pull them off.

A last check in the mirror shows that, sadly enough, my freckles have not melted away and my mop of reddish-brownish-blackish hair (Mom likes to tell me that my hair just couldn't decide which part of the family it wanted to look like.) has started frizzing out, as per usual. Not a big surprise. Someday I'm going to live somewhere without humidity. I apply just a bit more lip gloss, check my teeth, and pop my last breath mint. This is it.

I come out of the bathroom and still no Aubrey. I should have asked him where he was coming from so I'd have some idea when he'd arrive. I grab a booth toward the back, where I can see anyone coming through the door, private enough so that when he does arrive, it'll be nice and secluded. Perfect.

Fifteen minutes later and I've:

a) rearranged and color-coded all the sweetener packets,

b) ripped a napkin into teeny tiny shreds and subsequently pocketed the shreds, hiding them in the pocket of my too-tight jeans, to the great amusement of the guy sitting next to me (voyeuristic jerk), and

c) been asked three times by a snotty blond waitress if I wouldn't like something while I was waiting, because she thinks she's going to get stiffed on the tip by a teenager. Which she might. Since she's being snotty.

Aubrey finally comes in the door twenty minutes later and peers around the café looking adorably confused until I start waving my arms in an uncomfortably close imitation of Raven the Goth Girl. He sees me and comes over with a meltingly hot smile. Even the snotty waitress takes notice and straightens her little bow tie. She won't be so snippy when she comes over next time, I'll bet.

"Hey, Tina," he says as he sits down.

Okay, so he's way late *and* he can't get my name right. But man, is he hot. "Uh, actually, it's Mina. But lots of people do that, don't worry about it." Way too many people, actually. But it would have been really nice if the cutest guy ever hadn't done it.

He doesn't look remotely worried about it. "Right," he says. "Mina." He smiles vaguely at me and runs a hand through his hair so it flops perfectly over his forehead. "So, Mina, what's it been like living with vampires all this time? What are your parents like?"

Out of all the things that I had potentially thought we might talk about, my parents were not on the list. I figured maybe school would come up, or our impending decision on vampirism, maybe, or even (hopefully) something like, Gee, Mina, you sure do look hot in those jeans.

"Oh, well, they're pretty normal actually. I mean, they have regular jobs and everything. They aren't any weirder than anyone else's parents or anything." After all, everybody thinks their

50

parents are weird to some extent. I just happen to know exactly what my parents' particular weirdnesses are.

I didn't say anything that funny, but he laughs, showing off all his sparkling white teeth and I melt a little more. And I'm not the only one. I swear that I saw the waitress fan herself out of the corner of my eye. I ignore her in the hope that she backs off for a while. At least he's finally here and we're talking.

I rack my brain for something else clever to say. "Dad does say he's a Type AB Negative kind of guy." Actually, he says that as a joke sometimes when he's hanging out with Uncle Mortie. I don't know that you can really tell the difference between the blood types. Maybe you can. Maybe he hasn't been kidding about that all these years.

"Really?" Aubrey leans forward a little and I catch a whiff of musky cologne. Like he needed any more animal magnetism.

"Yeah, and my mom sometimes makes this nasty English dish called black pudding. It's got pig's blood in it, though, not human." Geez, at least that's what she told me. She wouldn't have fed me real human blood, would she? No. No. I'm sure she wouldn't.

"Oh? So they eat?"

"My uncle Mortie says there's no reason not to enjoy food." Man, and he certainly does enjoy it. He's just lucky that vampires

51

don't gain weight. He'd be at least three hundred pounds by now if it weren't for that.

Aubrey leans forward even more. I can see the flecks of gold and amber in his green eyes. He's so close I could lean forward just the tiniest bit and kiss him. I don't do it, but just thinking about it gives me a warm feeling and I blush. He doesn't seem to notice. He probably has that effect on all the girls.

"So your uncle is a vampire too?"

"What? Oh, yeah. Actually, he's the one that turned my dad and mom." Shouldn't we be talking about something else? Like . . . us? "And he's my sponsor."

"Wonderful. I'd love to meet him. And your parents. Maybe I could come over for dinner sometime?"

Wow. Whew. This isn't going anything like I thought it would. He wants to meet my parents already? And my uncle? Do boys normally want to meet your uncle? I think not. But it has to be good that he wants to come over for dinner, right? I've never invited anyone over for dinner before. Except Serena, but she doesn't count.

"I'm free this Sunday," he continues when I don't say anything right off.

I guess he's a proactive kind of guy. "Okay, I'll check with my mom. But are you sure you wouldn't rather, you know, go to a movie or something instead?"

The waitress picks that minute to interrupt. I bet she was listening in, the snotty thing. "Hi," she simpers, "can I get you anything?" She's staring soulfully into Aubrey's eyes and totally ignoring me. "Anything at all?" Her hand flutters suggestively over her chest. That is *so-o-o-o-o* obvious.

"How about a couple of lattes," he says politely, and turns back to me without even another glance at Ms. Snotty-pants. Yes! Though he could have asked first. I'm really more of a straight espresso kind of girl. I mean, if you're going for the caffeine high, you might as well be committed to it. "So, do you think Sunday will be okay with your parents?" The waitress wanders off looking disappointed. I wonder if she'll even remember to get the lattes.

"I'm pretty sure," I say. I can't imagine why Mom would say no. Shoot, she'll probably be all excited. It's not every day her little girl brings home the hottest guy in town.

"Great, here's my number." He pulls out an actual card and hands it to me. Talk about prepared.

"Wow, were you a boy scout or something?" I tease him.

He looks confused, which is a very cute look for him. As if any look wouldn't be cute on him.

"I just meant that you were prepared."

"Oh, I get it." He laughs. "It's a calling card like they used to use in the old days. You ever read Melman? Brighton Powell started using them back in *True Love Has Teeth*. I thought they sounded cool. Besides, they make it easier when people ask for my number. I've got my cell and my e-mail on there. It's best to call, though. I don't spend a lot of time online."

I don't understand half of what he's talking about, but it does make me wonder how many times he gets asked for his digits. I'm betting a lot. I bet if I left him alone for even five minutes that waitress would be on him like a bee on honey. Or is that a fly? Whatever, she'd be stuck on him like glue.

"Well, I'll give you a call later after I check with my mom. I'm sure it will be fine."

"Great," he says again and gets up. "I can't actually stay for the lattes, but please let me cover them." Before I can say anything, he pulls out some bills and lays them on the table. "Hope to see you Sunday." And then he's gone.

"Bye." I call out to the rapidly closing door.

The waitress drops off the lattes. "Where'd your friend rush off to?" she asks with no trace of the sweetness she'd had earlier while talking to Aubrey.

"He had to go," I say, even though I have no idea why he took off so fast either. It's none of her business anyway.

She looks at me speculatively. "He's not that actor, is he?"

I'm not sure which one she means, since technically it could be any number of actors. He *is*, after all, just that hot. I briefly consider telling her he is, but I'm not a liar at heart.

"Nah," I say and then pretend to look carefully around the place like I want to make sure no one is listening in. I lean forward and so does she. "He's that singer," I whisper.

Okay, so I am a little bit of a liar.

10:35 P.M.

SereneOne: soooo…how'd it go?

MinaMonster: idk. kinda weird

SereneOne: weird?

MinaMonster: yah. he kept askin bout the fam

MinaMonster: & he jetted prtty fast outta there. didn't evn drnk the coffee

SereneOne: ??

MinaMonster: i know, rite? but he's coming 4 dinner on sunday

SereneOne: omg!!! no way! i have 2 come by and see this Greek God!

MinaMonster: no can do. this 1 is mine! :-P

WHY IT SUCKS TO BE ME, CONTINUED

1. Sexy guys are mysteriously more interested in my family than they are in me. What is up with that?

2. I forgot to turn in that stupid Form 1060-something to G.W. on Tuesday and she called Mom to tell her that "I'm not taking my decision as seriously as I should be."

3. I actually lost the stupid form, so I will have to grovel after today's session so she'll give me a new one, plus some stupid Form 1080D she told Mom I'd have to fill out since I didn't get the first form in on time.

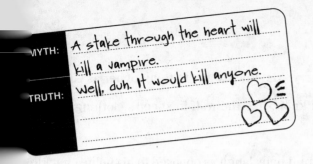

MYTH: A stake through the heart will kill a vampire.

TRUTH: well, duh. It would kill anyone.

7

Amazingly, I run into George five times in the hallway between classes. It turns out we have three classes right next door to each other. I have no idea how I never met him before. He even has World History right next door to my English class. I must totally zone normally.

"Ms. Tweeter, huh? I've heard she's a hoot. I've got Simpson for senior English and he's completely boring."

"You have no idea," I say. "You won't believe it, but we're doing *Dracula* now and she's been dressing up every day as a different character."

"Too funny," says George. "If she only knew—"

I cut him off, which is rude yeah, but he really needs to get a grip on the whole "Don't Tell" policy. "Um, yeah. Anyway, we still on for the tutoring session tonight before G.W.?"

"G.W.?"

"Oh, yeah, sorry. Ms. Riley. I like to think of her as Grandma Wolfington. You know, like the wolf in sheep's clothing kind of thing."

He gives his mini-belly laugh as opposed to his polite chuckle. It's pretty easy to classify his level of enjoyment. I give the "G.W." a four on a scale of ten.

"I like that." he says. "I'll see you tonight."

Today Ms. Tweeter is dressed up as Van Helsing. At least, that's my guess. She's got this weird Sherlock Holmes cap on and a long tweed overcoat (where she found that in California is anyone's guess). The crowning touch is a big wooden stake stuck in the back pocket of her khakis. I wonder if I should be insulted just on principle.

"Just a reminder," says Ms. Tweeter, in a bizarre accent that sounds vaguely Scottish or possibly Hungarian, "your term paper ideas are due tomorrow. I'm also going to be splitting you into teams of two for a group project on *Dracula*. We're going to do that the diplomatic way by picking names out of a hat, so no grumbling." She pulls the hat off her head and has everyone write their names on a slip of paper and drop it in.

I can't believe she's piling this much work on us so close to the end of the year. Geez, obsess much, Ms. Tweeter? I think she's got a serious thing for fangs and capes or something. And a group project? Double ugh.

I cross my fingers. Please, please, please don't let me get Bethany. The last time I had to work with her on a group project, it got *really* ugly and I got detention. Which really stunk, since she got detention too, and then I was stuck sitting in detention with her. Which wound up getting us both extended detention.

"If you pick a name from the hat of someone that already has a partner, just pick a new name. Justin Zabrowski, you're up first." That's the sucky thing about having a last name right in the middle of the alphabet. Even if a teacher like Ms. Tweeter goes wild and reverses the order from the normal A to Z, you're always stuck in the middle. I cheer silently when Mark Vail draws Bethany's name. I'm home free.

We make it all the way to my name without anyone picking me. Serena's already been chosen (she got Tim, sucks to be her) and Mark's stuck with Bethany, so I don't really care who I get. I reach my hand into the hat and hand the slip to Ms. Tweeter without even looking at it.

"Nathan Able," she reads off.

Whoa. I just make it back to my seat. Serena gives me a not-very-well-hidden big thumbs-up and a grin to match. I hope Nathan didn't notice. It had totally not occurred to me that I could get Nathan as a partner. Things never work out that way for me. Maybe I really am at a turning point in my life. First Aubrey asks me out and now this. I'm finally having some luck in the guy department.

We split out into our teams for the second half of the class. I give Nathan a weak smile and pray that my hair hasn't gone completely puffball. Now my problem is going to be getting through the project at all, because my tongue gets totally tied whenever I'm in close proximity to him. It's something about his eyes (warm, chocolatey, velvety brown) or maybe his hair (classic Californian blond with natural sun streaks) or maybe just the whole package (built, but not too built; thin, but not too thin; and a butt that I think even my mom would look at twice).

"Hey, Mina," he says. "I guess we're working together."

"Yeah," I say. Brilliant answer. I'm sure to stun him with my dazzling wit. I have *got* to pull it together. I remind myself that I actually carried on a conversation with a hot guy just yesterday. A short one, but still. A short conversation, that is. Aubrey's pretty tall.

"Well, you have any ideas?"

60

"I hadn't really thought about it," I admit. And just now I'm having a hard time concentrating because he's looking at me with those beautiful puppy-dog eyes. "But I'm sure the weirder the better, as far as Tweeter is concerned." I give him what I hope is a cute nonthreatening smile. "I know I can do weird, no problem, but are you even capable of being anything other than perfect?" Okay, maybe that was a little too thick, but he laughs, which is a good sign

"I'm sure I can manage. I was thinking we could do a reading from the book? Maybe even pick out something weird and unexpected or work in scenes *From Dusk Till Dawn* or some other vampire movies? Like a compare and contrast kind of thing? What do you think?" He grins at me.

"Sure." I smile back. "I *love* Tarantino. And we could get all dressed up and kind of act it out. I bet Tweeter would love that. Maybe even spray some fake blood around or something."

We sit and chat for the rest of class about all the stupid vampire movies we've seen and how Tarantino is a genius. We actually have a lot of movie stuff in common, which I wouldn't have guessed. I'd have thought he would be more of a normal action flick kind of guy. Best of all, he agrees with me that a *Sin City* sequel is worth camping out for and that Clive Owen has got to be in it.

61

I manage to:

a) actually speak in (mostly) complete sentences,

b) not say anything incredibly stupid, and

c) get Nathan's e-mail address and phone number. Woo-hoo!

I am definitely turning over a new leaf here.

Despite the fact that Dad dropped me off early, George is already sitting outside the community center when I arrive. I'm guessing that the assortment of oddball adults filtering out are from the adult version of the "Phlebotomy Club." They look too secretive to be coming from a flower arranging class.

"So," he says, "Whaddaya wanna know?"

"I don't know." I counter. "What did I miss?"

"Mostly vampire history, honestly. She went over the whole thing from the very first vampire back in the twelfth century to today, ad nauseum." He hands me a notebook. "It's all in here."

"Good, I'm glad I missed that." I glance through a few pages of the notebook. "I just can't believe you took notes."

"It was the only way I could stay awake."

I know the feeling. History is my worst subject. Once the teacher starts in on all the dates and place names and stuff like that, my brain goes completely numb.

"She's not actually going to test us on this stuff, is she?" Flipping through the notebook, I can tell it's really full of detail. He takes good notes. And doodles a lot. I notice one pretty good caricature of Grandma Wolfington pacing the room and yapping. She really does look kind of wolfish.

"Oh, God, I hope not," he says. "I wrote it down, but heck if I actually remember any of it. And there's no way I'm rereading it. It was boring enough the first time around."

"How did you get involved with all of this anyway?"

"In what?"

"The whole vampire thing. Ms. Riley made it sound like no one else had any vampire relatives. And it's not like they advertise or anything."

"Oh." He turns quiet a minute like he's thinking about it. "You're right. I don't have any vampire relatives. I don't have any relatives at all, actually."

It's my turn to say it. "Oh." I wish I hadn't asked. I never know how to react when people give me sob stories. Ugh, no. I don't mean to make it sound like that, like I think their problem is trivial. I totally don't. I just mean that when people lay it all out, I don't know how to react. You don't want to say, "Oh, I'm sorry", because it seems all fake. Everybody says that. So I usually wind up where I am right now, not saying anything at all.

"It's okay," he says. "I'm used to it. My parents died when I was six, so I don't really remember them too much. They were both only children and my grandparents died before I was even born."

"How did your parents die?" A nosy question, but I can't help but ask.

"A drunk driver ran into their car. They were coming back from dinner. The babysitter had to tell me. I've been living in foster care since then."

"Oh." I say again, like a total idiot.

He grins at me. "Sorry you asked, huh?"

"Yes! I mean, no . . . well, kind of. I'm really sorry." Ack, said it anyway. I'm such a dork.

He gives a self-deprecating chuckle. "No one ever knows what to say. Don't worry about it."

Wow, he seems like he really has a good handle on things. I have no idea what I would feel like if something like that had happened to me, but I can pretty much guarantee that I wouldn't be taking it as well as he is. You still don't want to bring up my first, and last, pet fish with me. Splashy's buried in the garden in a nice shady spot with a hand-carved wooden marker (well, okay, a hand-lettered block of wood, but I did use really good penmanship) that says, Here Lies Splashy. May He Swim in Peace Forevermore. Amen.

"Anyway, I'd never really thought about being a vampire or

anything like that, but I met this one crazy kid at the last foster home I was in. Well, I guess he wasn't really crazy, since he was dead on, but he talked all the time about vampires being real and stuff like that. Then one day he just disappeared. That's not really all that unusual since kids like him run away all the time. But he left me a note about where to find him. And so I looked him up one day when I was feeling bored and he'd been turned. And I thought, why the heck not?"

"So that's all there is to it, huh?"

He gives me another impish grin. "Well, if you want to get all psychological, I guess you could say I'm trying to compensate for the untimely death of my parents by living forever. But I'm really not that deep."

I doubt that somehow, but I don't argue. "So where do you live now?" I mentally give myself another smack for being nosy. He's just so easy to talk to.

"I've been in the system long enough to know how to work it, so when I heard they had a larger vampire community here, I wrangled a move and a place by myself. I was close enough to eighteen that they approved it. Honestly, I think they were probably glad to get rid of me."

"So you live all by yourself?" That blows my mind. But, I guess, I'll be doing that soon enough myself. Still, it's really weird to know someone in high school doing it. I mean, how do you live? Who cooks dinner and does the laundry?

"Yeah. I've got a part-time job at a bookstore and the government helps subsidize the housing. It's no big deal."

"How come you were never adopted?" Wow, I should really buy myself a muzzle or something. I'm obviously going for Nosy Nellie of the Year.

He doesn't seem to mind the question, thankfully. He laughs again, this time his mid-range goofy chuckle. "I was a rotten kid. I didn't want to be adopted at first because I didn't believe my parents were really gone. And then it got to be like a game. You know, how many pranks could I pull before this family gave up on me and things like that."

"Oh, I'm sure you weren't that bad." I can't imagine him being that mean. He really seems pretty nice once you get to know him. And way more fun than I would have thought. He looks so *normal*. But, I guess, how normal can you be when you're thinking about becoming a vampire?

"You have no idea," he says. "I was terrible. I grew out of it after a while, but by then it was too late. Once you're past twelve or so, there's very little hope you'll get adopted. Now, how about you? I know your parents are vampires, but how did you wind up in the vampire sessions now? You're a junior, right? Most of us

66

are seniors and a couple people graduated last year."

"Well, The Council didn't actually know about me until recently. My parents never exactly told them they had a kid. And now that they know . . . "

I was about to explain about the whole Uncle Mortie fiasco when Lorelai sweeps into the room, pulls me out of my chair with a quick, "Sorry, George, girl business," and bundles me off to a corner of the room. I give George a shrug and wiggle my fingers at him, which he hopefully takes as, Thanks a lot and talk to you later, okay?

"Girl," she shrieks, "you totally did not call me! What happened with Aubrey yesterday?"

I had completely forgotten about calling Lorelai. In fact, I have no idea what I even did with her number.

"Sorry! I completely forgot. It was pretty low key. He couldn't stay long." She looks immeasurably disappointed for someone who barely knows me. "But he did ask if he could come over for dinner on Sunday." She perks right up.

"Ohmigod! That's huge! What did you guys talk about?"

"Nothing, really. He mostly just asked about my family."

She simmers down again, looking a little confused. "That's weird. Who cares about that stuff? He didn't mention what you were wearing or anything like that? You did wear something decent, right?"

I shrug my shoulders. I had already decided that I wasn't going to worry about the why's or wherefore's and just enjoy it. It's not every day that some sexy guy asks me out. Not even every other day. Generally, I'm a magnet for losers, geeks, and members of the band.

"Oh well," she says. "You better call me Sunday night after dinner. Remember this time!"

I nod and make a mental note to search through my backpack once I get home for her number. That's usually where anything I lose winds up. I don't know what I'll do when I'm out of school and stuck with a dinky purse. I have way too much stuff for that. I'll be like one of those old women carrying around a beach tote or a duffel bag.

I'm about to head back and apologize to George for ditching him (not like I had a choice) when Aubrey walks in and heads in my direction. Lorelai gives a little squeal and runs off so I can be alone with him. One thing you gotta give to cheerleaders, they know what to do about boys. No question about that. But she could definitely be a little less obvious.

"Hi, Mina," he says. Thank God he didn't call me Tina again.

"Hey, Aubrey." I manage to croak out. I clear my throat so hopefully he'll think I have a cold or something instead of just being the dateless dork that I am.

"So, are we on for dinner on Sunday?"

"Yep, everything's cool with my parents." My mom was actually surprisingly cool about it, considering that Sunday is technically a school night. She asked me if he was cute (Dad cringed), and when I told her just how cute, she gave me a high five. Mom is awesome.

"Here's my address. Around sixish?" Maybe I'm a little like my dad, since I was anal enough to write it all out for Aubrey. Or maybe I'm just anxious. I could have just called, but I thought it would give me an excuse to chat with him in person if I waited.

"Great," he says and wanders off with a little wave. And that was it. I guess he's not much for chatting. Hopefully he won't just wander off in the middle of dinner on Sunday.

I look back at George, but he's not looking my way at all. In fact, he's deep in conversation with Linda with his back turned to me. I'll have to thank him for the notes later.

I take a seat next to Lorelai and fill her in on the latest development with Aubrey. Admittedly, it wasn't a long conversation, but she congratulates me anyway and shoots a dirty look at Raven, who just wandered in.

"I'm so glad he's cozying up with you instead of Raven," she says.

"Why?" I'm not real fond (obviously) of Goth Girl myself, but I have to admit she probably isn't really that bad. Maybe. And I can totally appreciate why she's so protective of Aubrey.

"Because she's got such a chip on her shoulder about the whole vampire thing. She acts like she's better than all of us. Says she's been 'practicing' for years."

I snort. "Practicing? Is that what she calls prancing around in that Goth getup? I've got news for her. None of the vampires I know dress anything like that."

"Good thing," says Lorelai, "it would totally clash with my cheerleading outfit."

I'm about to laugh when I realize she's serious. Man, I'm just not used to cheerleaders. I never know when they are joking and when they are serious. It's like they speak another language, Cheerleaderease. Luckily, Grandma Wolfington picks that moment to come in.

"Today we're going to talk about vampire law. Some of these laws are officially set down by the Councils while others are just commonly understood. You will all be expected to follow these laws without question." She gives a stern look around the room to emphasize the point.

"Arguably the most important and inviolate law is that you must never, ever reveal that you are a vampire to a human." I notice she looks right at me. Great. I resist the urge to give her a thumbs-up. I guess that's why I had to pretend I hadn't known about my parents and Uncle Mortie. I wonder what they would do if they knew my parents had broken that law years ago?

"In keeping with that, you must also not turn a human without first having consulted with The Council and sponsoring the human as a candidate."

Between those two right there, how in the world are new vampires ever created? And that sure isn't what happened to Uncle Mortie. He was blindsided by the whole thing. He never went through any silly vampire lessons.

George holds his hand up and Grandma Wolfington nods at him. "What happens to those that break those laws? I have definitely heard of cases where one or both of those rules were broken."

Hmmm, yeah, that weird friend he was telling me about, for one. And everyone in my family, but I'm not volunteering that to the class.

"They are dealt with," she says menacingly. Looking at her, I don't doubt it. I wonder what happened to the vampire that turned Uncle Mortie? Did they do anything to her? Man, I better make sure I don't slip up and say anything about my parents.

"Well," he continues, "how do normal humans find about

71

vampirism then? If you can't talk to anyone about it, how do we ever get new vampires? I mean, vampires can't have children, so if no one gets turned . . . " Yes! My question exactly! I give George an eyebrow wiggle for encouragement. We must be on the same wavelength.

Grandma Wolfington gives him a deep look like she's trying to determine whether he's a troublemaker or what. I'm not sure what she decides, but she starts pacing the room with long strides. "There are always those humans that believe in us, no matter what they learn in school. Those humans always find a way to reach out to us and many of them are accepted. Some of you in here today fall under that category. And yes, there are instances where the laws have been broken."

She stops pacing. "But you must remember something. We do not actively recruit new vampires. We are limited in number and must remain that way. After all, we live so long that if there were hundreds of thousands of us, it would be noticeable. When there are few, we can blend in more easily." She turns and looks right at George and then at each of us in turn. "Always remember that vampires *can* be killed. Humans can be many things to us: friends, lovers, enemies, prey, but if our secret were widely known, we would be hunted."

No one says a word. When she puts it like that, it all sounds so deadly serious. Do I really want to be hated? I mean, if people knew? And prey? I can't imagine ever thinking of the kids I go to school with as prey, not even Bethany, as much as I'd like something horrible to befall her. Like a plague of zits that never go away or toilet paper stuck to her shoe. But not anyone actually hunting her down to chow on.

"Anyway, continuing on, we do not kill if we can avoid it. Unnecessary deaths draw attention that we do not want."

Yikes! That certainly implies that there may be unavoidable deaths, doesn't it? Ohmigod. I am *so* not killing someone.

"Following on with that, just be discreet in general. Do not flaunt your powers or anything that might peg you as a vampire."

It's obvious that she's never been at our house for Halloween and seen Uncle Mortie all dressed up. I bet he'd get a talking to. I'm very sure he hasn't killed anyone, though. Except maybe with bad jokes.

"Those are the most important laws to follow. There are many more that have to do with how the vampire community is run, how the Council members are chosen, and what they are in charge of. I've prepared a pamphlet for you." She hands them out to us.

She's big on these brochure-pamphlet things. This one is quite thick and looks to be some really dry reading.

"I expect you to read through the pamphlet by our next session."

Great, vampire homework on top of my regular homework.

Grandma Wolfington spends the rest of the session talking about the proper not-against-the-rules ways to obtain blood, which kind of grosses me out. The easiest way seems to be to stop by a vampire "watering hole" that's essentially a blood bar. I'm not at all sure how *they* get the blood though. Ew. I don't really want to think about that. I guess it's better than attacking someone in a dark alley though.

She even mentions that some vampires live wholly off of animal blood and there are butcher vampires across the world where you can stock up discreetly. Good to know it doesn't have to be human blood. That's one discussion I've never had with my parents. I never really wanted to know where they get their blood. Hopefully they're just the animal-blood-drinking variety of vampire. They keep a fridge down in the basement, but I never go in it.

G.W. wraps things up with another dire warning to not break any of the rules. She never mentions what the specific "or else" is, but that's another thing I think I'd be perfectly happy not knowing.

"And lastly, be sure to contact your sponsor and check

in. They should have some activities planned for the coming week." This time, she looks at me. "And if they don't, please let me know."

Knowing Uncle Mortie, our planned activity will probably involve either:

a) food,

b) hot chicks, or

c) food and hot chicks.

I still can't believe he's my sponsor.

I get stuck talking to G.W. about the importance of filling out all forms on time, no matter what and don't get to do more than wave good-bye to Aubrey or George. The woman has been a vampire for so long her blood must have gone to dust years ago.

11:22 P.M.

MinaMonster: u have any idea for ur paper yet?

SereneOne: yah, im psyched. im gonna.do a study of the vampire legends in Romania.

SereneOne: i chckd out some cool books from the library

MinaMonster: sweet

SereneOne: u?

MinaMonster: derno. gonna read a lil more
and c if anything hits me

SereneOne: nothing like leaving it to the
last minute...

MinaMonster: yah, yah, thx mom

Too bad I can't give Serena all those notes I got from George. She'd probably get an F though, since no one would believe any of it was true. Not even Tweeter.

8

I stayed up half the night reading that stupid book and the more I read, the more pissed off I got. Where did Bram Stoker get off on calling women weak and no-good? I mean, it's Mina that does all the work and actually pieces everything together, and Van Helsing and her stupid husband Jonathan just take all the credit. I am so pissed. I can't believe Ms. Tweeter is having us read this propaganda.

At least I know what I'm going to write about for my term paper now. Something about the women in the book getting the shaft and no pun intended there either. Yeah, Lucy was a total twit, but all her boyfriends sure didn't have any trouble killing her once she was an 'evil' vampire. Shoot, she had more personality as a vampire than as a person anyway. Ugh.

I know, I know, I probably wouldn't be this worked up about

it if I didn't have my own big vampire question hanging over my head.

All the stuff I'm learning in the vampire sessions is kind of intriguing. Granted, G.W. is totally toeing the party line and doesn't really talk about any of the bad stuff. (Well, except for humans potentially wanting to stamp out all vampires if they knew they were real.) And I know that vampires aren't hideously ugly or evil like in *Dracula* or the movies. Okay, Uncle Mortie isn't exactly a pretty boy, but Mom is definitely better than average. Not that looks are the most important thing. Gah!

All I'm trying to say is that maybe it wouldn't be the end of the world to be a vampire. The end of your life, yeah, kind of. But not the end of the world.

On the ride to school in the Death Beetle, Serena bubbles on and on about all the Romanian vampire legends she's been reading. I'm dying to tell her which ones are true and which ones aren't (I actually read some of George's notes last night whenever Stoker was really pissing me off). I've always been horrible at keeping information to myself. Dad says it's my giving nature. Mom says I'm just a blabbermouth. I hope she didn't tell The Council that.

Nothing exciting happens all day until after English. (Ms. Tweeter totally dug our project idea and was even all over the idea of a Tarantino tie-in.)

Nathan pulls me aside and says, "Hey Mina, we're all going out for pizza tomorrow for lunch. You want to come?" Serena, standing right behind him, starts dancing a little jig and high-fiving the air. I try to act all cool like I get asked to hang with the popular kids every day.

"Sure. Sounds cool. Um, Serena's free too . . ." That causes even more happy dancing behind Nathan's back. She's so totally not a Goth girl. A true Goth girl wouldn't care about going out for pizza with the in crowd.

"Sure. We're meeting at Chili Pepper's at noon. See you then." He turns to go and Serena just barely stops her jiggity-jig in time. "Oh, and see you there too, Serena."

"Works for me," she says, totally copying my cool-as-a-cucumber new attitude.

We make it all the way to her car before we totally lose it.

"Ohmigod," Serena shrieks. "What am I going to wear?"

"You mean I might get you out of that Goth girl getup for once?" Bonus!

"Well, it just doesn't seem like a Chili Pepper's kind of thing," she says sheepishly.

I have been working on her for over a year to give up on the all-black ultra-depressing wardrobe. Who knew it would just take a pizza place and Nathan Able to do it.

"Do you think Chris Rink will be there?"

Now the truth comes out. I had no idea she had a thing for Chris Rink. Admittedly, he's pretty hot. Not quite up to Nathan standards, but quite yummy. But he's an out-and-out jock who plays both basketball and baseball.

"I didn't think you went for the jock type," I tease her. Serena blushes bright red, truly a hard thing to do underneath all that Goth makeup.

"A girl can dream, can't she?"

"No reason not to dream," I say. I look her up and down. It's been ages since I've seen it, but I know she's got it going on under all those layers of black clothes. "Let's go over to my place and get all that gunk off of you. Maybe Mom will take us shopping. I think this calls for new outfits all around. I've been saving up my allowance and I bet Mom'd front us some money."

Like I said before, I'm not really a girly girl. But I'll take a good excuse to go shopping anytime, especially if it involves getting Serena into something not black.

Mom is all over the shopping trip when she hears that Serena is coming out of her Goth shell. She hated the whole look even more than I did. She even buys us some new non-Goth makeup on top of a new outfit each, which is a total splurge that I'm sure

80

Dad is going to have a fit over later. Sometimes she treats Serena more like my sister than my best friend, but she knows that Serena's mom probably won't even notice that she's dropped the Goth look. Her dad is okay, but her mom is a total witch . . . and I'm just leaving off the *b* to be polite.

We drop Serena off at her house with a load of shopping bags and pick up Chinese for dinner on the way home.

"Two dates in one weekend," Mom says as we're getting out of the car. "My little girl is growing up."

Oh wow, I'd almost forgotten about Aubrey. Yee-haw! Two hot guys in two days! I have so turned over a new leaf. I just smile smugly. I'll even forgive her for the cheesy commentary.

"That reminds me," says Mom. "We need to talk about a few things."

Gah. There's a total downer. "What kind of things?" I hope G.W. didn't call again. I made sure to fill out those stupid forms as soon as I got home last night.

"Oh, it'll wait until after dinner."

So of course I spend all dinner obsessing over what she could possibly want to talk about. My grades—doing fine. Vampire lessons—going okay. Uncle Mortie—no word yet. My room—decently clean. Nothing I come up with prepares me for the actual conversation.

"Okay," says Mom, after all the dishes are safely tucked away in the dishwasher. "Let's talk about sex."

Did I mention my mom doesn't mess around with getting to the point? I'm just glad Dad wasn't in the room. He'd have totally choked.

"Uh, Mom . . . " I manage to stutter out. "I kind of know the whole birds and bees thing. Dad gave me that one years ago." And it is still, to this day, one of my most horrifying memories. A true accountant, he had charts and everything. Frightening. It's amazing I'm not a complete emotional basket case after that.

"No, no," she says, "I'd be very surprised if you didn't know something about the birds and the bees by now. After all, you're almost seventeen. I mean sex as a vampire. If you decide to turn. I thought I'd take this topic on instead of Uncle Mortie."

"Oh. Um, thanks." Well, that's a new one for me and definitely something that hadn't crossed my mind. I mean, sure, sex crosses my mind (I am a teenager!), but I hadn't given any thought about the specifics of, you know, vampire sex. And learning about it from Uncle Mortie? The very thought is disgusting.

"First of all, vampires can and do have sex. In fact, your dad and I found that sex got even better in some ways after we turned. You develop muscles in all kinds of unexpected places."

"Mom!" Oh ugh, the pictures going through my head! I am so grossed out right now. If she just hadn't added that bit about the muscles, I might have been able to contain my grossed-outedness, but oh man.

"Oh come on," Mom laughs, "you know we have sex. Your father and I love each other. Where do you think you came from?"

"Knowing something and actually thinking about something are two entirely different things. I prefer to think I came from the stork, if I have to think about it at all."

She just laughs. But I bet she'd be grossed out if she thought about her mother having sex. Oh God, I shouldn't have thought of that. Now I've got images of my grandparents running around naked in my head. I don't know which is worse: images of Mom and Dad or Gran and Gramps. I try thinking about G.W. reciting all of the vampire laws, one by one. In detail. Annotated.

"I just want you to know that you wouldn't be missing out on anything in the sex department." She stops laughing finally and turns serious on me. "But, you would be missing out on the experience of childbirth and the joy of having children. I'm very thankful that I was able to experience both before turning."

"I've never really thought about having kids," I say. It's true. I know some girls have their weddings all planned out and the names of their first kid all picked, but I've never been into that.

My dreams have been more about traveling the world visiting exotic locales. Things like that. And childbirth, uh, don't think I'll mind missing out on that one. I saw that movie *Knocked Up*. Ee-e-ew. I had to close my eyes a couple of times.

"It's a hard choice to have to make so young. I just don't want you to regret whatever decision you make. I don't regret my choice, but I know that you might not choose the same path. I just want to make sure you know what your options are."

I give her a hug and allow myself to give in a little to the pity party we've got going on. "I just wish I didn't have to choose now," I whine. "Why are they making me decide now?"

Mom looks at me a minute like she's deciding whether or not she should say anything. She opens and closes her mouth a few times and then sighs. "For one thing, we can't go on being your parents for very much longer."

"Excuse me?" What, they want to disown me now?

"Sorry, honey, that didn't come out right. You see, it's a matter of age. I mean, you may not have noticed, but we really haven't aged since we were turned. It's getting pretty hard to pass as your parents any more."

I take a really good look at Mom. She's right. I never really thought about it, but she could practically pass for my older sister. She was pretty young when she had me and she turned right after that. The last time we went to a movie, I swear the popcorn guy was flirting with her and not me. That, let me tell you, is not good for the ego.

"I've been adding some gray to my hair the last couple of years, but it's hard to add convincing wrinkles."

"So what are you saying?"

"Just that, one way or another, things will have to change. There's no way around it. It's about time to move before the neighbors get suspicious. The Council advises moving at least every ten years and we're way behind schedule. We wanted you to be able to stay with your friends in the same school system."

I think about nosy Mrs. Finch, who's always asking me how my mother is and asking things like what kind of moisturizer does she use and stuff like that. And then there's Mr. Jackson, my Chemistry teacher, who actually asked to see her ID once when she came for a parent-teacher conference.

She gives me a big squeeze. "But you'll always be my little girl. No matter what. I want you to know that."

"I know," I say.

It seems to me that there's an awful lot they still aren't telling me, but I don't want to ask the obvious question. I'm not sure I want to know what happens if I decide I don't want to be a vampire.

WHY IT SUCKS TO HAVE PARENTS WHO ARE VAMPIRES

1. Sneaking out or talking on the phone late at night is completely out when your parents can hear everything.

2. They never sleep, so you can't get away with anything at night.

3. Drinking (which I'm not a big fan of anyway, but it's not like I had a choice) is totally out, since they can also smell better than those bloodhounds the police use. Or sniff better. Whatever.

4. Lying is almost impossible, since they can detect even the tiniest variation in your pulse. It's like a built-in lie detector.

5. You have to remind them to buy food, since they don't eat. I started shopping for myself when I was thirteen. Though, the good news is that they don't always notice when I just eat cereal for dinner.

6. They make you choose between life and death. Literally.

9

Serena calls and wakes me up at 7:30 a.m. On a *Saturday*. The girl is just crazy. She knows me better than that. I never get up before at least nine on the weekend. Unless Christmas falls during that time. Yes, I still wake up early for Christmas.

"Mina, can I come over? So we can get dressed and go over to Chili Pepper's together?" I mumble something that must have sounded like an affirmative, because ten minutes later she's shaking me awake.

Happily, there's no trace of Goth makeup on her. But her face is almost as pale due to a case of extreme nerves. I've never seen her quite like this before. She dumps a bag containing what looks like every piece of clothing she owns out over the bed on top of me.

"I don't know what to wear!" she cries and flops down onto the bed, causing an avalanche of skirts and shirts to nearly bury me completely. I fight to clear a path to air.

"Why don't you just wear that new outfit that my mom just got you? It looks great on you." And it really did. A little red sundress with bright yellow and white flowers, it was such a far cry from her Goth get-up that it was just astounding. It made me cheerful just to look at her in it. I bet it would make Chris Rink full of cheer too.

Serena buries her head under a pink camisole and mumbles something unintelligible.

"What?"

She comes up for air and looks everywhere but at me. "I said"— big gulp of air—"I spilled something on it."

"How did you spill something on it? We just got it yesterday!"

She looks miserable, which is the only reason I don't laugh when she tells me, "I was practicing. And I got some tomato sauce on it."

"You were practicing?"

She finally looks right at me, a little defiantly. "Well, it was so much easier in the Goth stuff. As long as it was black, you were good to go. And I'm not used to being out with boys. Guys. You know."

"So, what, you go Goth for a year or two and now you've forgotten how to wear clothes?" I can't help it now. I let out a little laugh.

She looks like she's about to cry, but she finally starts laughing a little too. "I know, it sounds stupid. But I guess I have. I was thinking about getting out of the Goth stuff last year, but . . . "

"But you were too lazy to start picking out outfits again?"

She giggles a little. "Yeah, kind of."

I wish I'd known. I totally would have shown up at her house every morning to pick out her daily outfit to get her out of that Goth stuff. I would have even gotten up early to do that.

"You," I pronounce solemnly, "are a total goober." We both dissolve into another bout of giggles.

"But seriously, what am I going to wear?"

"Did you bring over the dress?"

"I think so . . . " She digs around in the pile for a while and finally comes up with success. The dress, as promised, has a huge tomato sauce stain right on the front.

"Geez, girl, what did you do? Bathe in spaghetti?"

"I accidentally leaned over into the serving bowl." That explains the position of the stain. Serena's a bit more endowed than I am.

"Ok, well, it was good you didn't put it through the dryer. That sets the stain. We've got a good chance of getting it out."

"You think?"

"Trust me." One of my few talents is removing stains. I have no idea how I learned how to do it, but I can get almost anything out of any kind of material. My Home Economics teacher would be so proud of me. I guess it could come in handy later on for removing blood spots. Ick. I push that thought right out of my head as fast as I can.

I rinse the spot clean with cold water from the inside of the dress out until no more sauce comes off. Then I soak the whole front of it in white vinegar for a good twenty minutes, with Serena trying to peek at it every two. Then a little dishwashing soap rubbed in for good measure, and I wash it in the washing machine in cold water. Presto-chango!. The dress comes out with no stain.

"Lucky you came over so early," I say, though I really could have used that extra sleep. I was tossing and turning last night after my little heart-to-heart with Mom.

But that's what friends are for. Serena once missed summer camp to keep me company when I had the flu. And she had a crush on one of the camp counselors at the time. That's true friendship.

The rest of the morning is taken up with applying makeup and doing our hair. I finally just do Serena's makeup myself because she keeps trying to put the blush and eye shadow on too heavy. It's going to take a while to acclimatize her to the real world again. We make it out the door with only a few minutes to spare to get over to Chili Pepper's Pizza Parlor.

It's a really cool place with this nice retro feel, like an old soda counter from the 1950s. A huge counter with the round swivel stools that you can spin around and around on dominates most of the place. I really loved those stools as a kid. I haven't been to Chili Pepper's lately though because:

a) It's where all the popular kids hang out and they stare at you with complete disdain when you try to eat there in all your glorious dweebosity,

b) I can't resist their chocolate banana milkshakes and they are so-o-o-o not good for the waistline, and

c) Hmmmm, well, I don't really have a good *c*. Maybe I've just been too chicken (see *a*).

All the A-list is clustered in the dead center of the long counter, with Nathan at the very epicenter. There must be at least thirty of them jostling for position. Ha! And they call vampires bloodsuckers.

I'm seriously considering backing out when Nathan sees us and waves us over.

"Hey, Mina. Serena? Wow, Serena, I like the new look! Here, I saved you some seats." He taps two football players on either side of him and they get up without a single grumble, pushing the next person in line down with a ripple effect. Then he pats the stools for us to sit down. We're getting the royal treatment. Serena looks at me wide-eyed from the other side of Nathan. I imagine I have a similar look on my face and try to wipe it off, probably unsuccessfully. The A-list conversations go on around us like nothing has happened, but I see a couple of people in the third row giving us dirty looks.

Nathan is chatting amiably with us about nothing in particular: how hard the last Chemistry test was (we all think we bombed it), Serena's new get up (loves the red dress, loves the hair, loves the whole thing), our English project (he can't wait to find a costume better than Ms. Tweeter's and show her up), and his cool new car (bright red Mini Cooper with a white stripe down the side).

I'm starting to wonder if the A-list doesn't actually eat after all, since no one is eating anything and we're surrounded by the heavenly smell of pepperoni and cheese. I knew I should have had breakfast, but there just wasn't any time in between emergency stain removal and makeup application. Chili Pepper's has a by-the-slice counter with over fifteen different pizzas to choose from, and each and every one of them is calling my name. My stomach is going crazy. This is one time when being a vampire would be handy. I can barely concentrate on the conversation I'm so hungry.

And then my stomach goes in knots as I see Bethany break rank from the fourth row (good to know she's not in the innermost circle) and saunter over to us.

"When did they start letting Goth-lovers in here, anyway?" she spits out, glaring at me. Okay, now, this is absolutely and totally unacceptable because

a) Serena isn't even dressed up in Goth stuff anymore, so obviously Bethany hasn't even really looked at us, and

b) I have never been a Goth-lover. It's not like I hung out with any Goth people other than Serena, and they wouldn't even hang out with her either since she wasn't a true black-hearted, Siouxsie and the Banshees-loving, Edgar Allan Poe-reading Goth, but even if I was, what business of hers was it anyway? And,

c) Have I mentioned how much I detest Bethany?

Before I can say anything, Nathan turns to look at Bethany with a polite but distant expression on his face. "Excuse me, Bethany? Did you say something? I thought I heard you say something. But I'm not sure, since I'm certain we weren't talking to you." I can hear A-listers all around us sucking in their breath in one collective *who-o-o-oa*.

Have I mentioned how much I love Nathan Able?

Bethany opens and closes her mouth a few times, but nothing comes out. She looks like a fish out of water. Nathan doesn't even appear to notice, as he goes back to chatting with Serena. I can't help a small snicker from escaping my lips. Bethany shoots me a look that could peel paint off the wall, but stands down without saying anything else and returns to her fourth-row spot, though the girl next to her backs off a little and starts talking to someone on her other side. If someone poured water on Bethany right about now (and oh, how I'd like to), it would come off as steam.

The football player who had vacated his seat for me introduces himself as Bo, short for Bobby, and goes into a highly detailed account of the pass route he executed on the single touchdown we scored in the last game of the season. I nod in what I think are all the right places, and I guess I'm doing okay since he doesn't stop talking. I am starting to feel absolutely faint with hunger.

Finally, some kind of A-list signal occurs and people start ordering pizza left and right. Before Serena and I can order, Nathan hands us slices of pizza with pepperoni, banana peppers, and sausage.

"My favorite," he says. "Hope you like it. If not, just let me know what you like and I'll get it for you. Anything you want, no problem."

I have no idea what we did to deserve the royal treatment, but I have no complaints. We tell him, "Thanks" and "We love it" (which I would have said even if it had liver and onions on it), and dig in. I devour the slice in approximately 2.6 seconds. Serena takes a more ladylike minute or two to get hers down. Nathan runs off to get us some more pizza with a chuckle and a comment about healthy appetites.

Serena leans over to me and whispers, "I always knew he was nice, but this is awesome."

"I know," I whisper back. "It's like heaven. And I loved the look on Bethany's face. That was priceless. I could live off that for a year."

Serena looks around a minute at the A-listers gathered around us. "What did we do to get here, anyway?"

I shrug. Never look a gift horse in the mouth. "I guess because I'm working on that English project with him. I dunno."

Nathan gets back and gallantly passes us two more slices of his favorite. I actually hate banana peppers, but there's no way I'm bringing that up right now. That's at least a third-date kind of admission. I don't want to give him any reason for not being glad he asked us to tag along.

"So," I say after I've devoured the second piece, "you guys come here often?"

Serena rolls her eyes at me behind Nathan's back. I know it's a cliché and I also know darn well they come here nearly every weekend, but I'm trying to work up to getting invited again.

Nathan seems oblivious to the corny nature of my question or maybe is just too polite to mention it. "Oh, yeah, we come here every Saturday for lunch. You guys should come again sometime."

Yes! Open invitation! Not exactly a romantic proposal or anything, but still. I'll take it.

"Cool," I say, like I get invitations to hang out with the A-list every day. "Maybe we will."

Nathan gives a little chuckle. If it had been George, it would have been his how-cute-are-you laugh. "You guys ever do anything separately?"

"We're a package deal," I say and give Serena a shoulder squeeze, managing to work my arm around Nathan's back to do it. If I'm getting an in, I don't want to leave her behind. I've seen that happen to other people, and it sucks. And if they don't want her too, then I don't want them. Friendship is more important than being on the A-list or even Nathan. No matter how cool they are. Or think they are. Bethany is *so* not cool in my book.

"Gotcha." He nods. "Well, we're going to my house after to hang out by the pool. You guys want to come along?"

"Oh yeah," says Serena. She's in recently un-Gothed popularity nirvana. Her eyes are all sparkly and everything. "I'll just need to swing by my house to get a suit."

This day keeps getting better and better. "Absolutely," I say. "Just let me check with my mom, she'd said to call her after this 'cause she had something for me to do. I'm sure it can wait though."

I duck outside and give Mom a call. I should have known better.

My luck is just not that good and things have been going way too well lately.

"Oh, honey," she says, "your uncle Mortie's here already. He says he's taking you somewhere."

"On a Saturday night?"

"I'll ask him if it can wait, but he's already been waiting about half an hour." She lowers her voice a little. "And he's driving me crazy, I tell you. The man can't entertain himself."

"Well, he didn't even tell me he was coming!"

She sighs. "You know your uncle Mortie. I'll go check with him."

I can't believe Uncle Mortie didn't tell me. Does he think I've got nothing better to do on a Saturday night than hang out with my weirdest relative? Okay, yeah, I don't normally have any-thing planned, but still. I could have. He should've at least asked me first.

Mom comes back to the phone. "Sorry, Mina, but he says it has to be tonight. He said it was something special."

I groan. "Ok, I'll be home in just a few."

Serena takes one look at my face when I go back in and goes, "Oh, no, what is it?"

"I can't go," I say glumly. "Have to do a thing with Uncle Mortie."

"Your weirdo uncle? Why? Can't it wait?"

"It's a family thing. I've got to go." Man, I *hate* not being able to tell her what's going on.

"Do you want me to go with you? I don't have to go to Nathan's, if you need me to come along and run interference," she says. See, that's how good of a friend she is. But it's not like I can have her tagging along with me and Uncle Mortie on our little vampire field trip.

"No, you go. You'll have fun. No reason for you to suffer too. Uncle Mortie is killing my social life, but we won't let him torch yours too."

I tell Nathan I can't come, but Serena can. He nods and tells me he'll see me Monday. "Maybe next time," he adds as I walk away.

That cheers me up a little at least. That definitely implies that there will actually be a next time. Whoo-hoo! But I could still kill Uncle Mortie. I'd much rather it was *this* time rather than next time. He's got horrible timing.

Serena drops me off on the way to grab her bathing suit. "It better not be black!" I tell her, and she's still laughing as she drives off.

Seriously, though, I'm totally going to check up on that. I want to make sure this un-Goth-ing thing sticks.

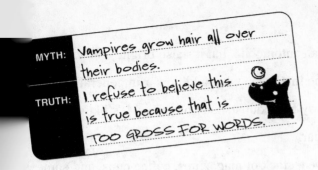

10

I find Uncle Mortie following my mom around the kitchen. It figures he would be, since she's baking cookies for her monthly Bunco outing. I guess I better get him out of there before she loses all her cookies (from him eating them, I mean, not her like literally losing her cookies. Or whatever. You know what I mean).

"Hey, Uncle Mortie," I say. "So what's the deal?"

"Oh, hey, Mina," he says as he sneaks another chocolate chip. "You ready to motor?"

I shrug. He might as well know I'm not exactly overjoyed at going out with him on a Saturday night. "Where are we going?"

"You'll see." He winks at me as Mom rolls her eyes. "C'mon, let's get going. Lots to do. Lots to see. Lots to eat." He leads the way to his car.

I hate riding with Uncle Mortie in his car. Not only is it an absolute boat of an automobile, but it's also bright yellow. Cadillacs should not be that color, ever, and no car in general should be this particularly obnoxious shade of yellow. It's like the sun threw up on the car.

I have to shove a stack of magazines, coffee cups, and some other unidentifiable stuff out of my way to get into the front seat. "Keep meaning to clean that up," Uncle Mortie says cheerfully. Yeah, sure. It's probably been this way since the 1970s when he bought the thing.

"So what have you learned so far in your little vampire lessons?"

"Well, the first one I went to was all about the physical changes. You know, strength, eyesight, blah, blah, blah."

"Did they tell you about hair?" Uncle Mortie turns onto the freeway and his car lets out an almost human-sounding wheeze of dismay.

Hair? Oh no, is that bit of folklore about vampires growing hair everywhere really true? Or the one about losing your hair? Maybe Mom and Dad have to shave all the time. Or wear wigs. "No, they didn't mention anything about hair. What about it?" I ask as calmly as I can.

"Oh nothing big, really. Just that it continues to grow. You'll still have to get it cut." He rubs his bald spot. "Too bad turning doesn't make it grow back though."

I breathe a sigh of relief. I would look hideous bald. Not that my hair is all that great, but it's still hair. And it would really have sucked to have to wear a wig. Or to have to shave like your whole body. I mean, how much time would that take? And the razor burn? Man.

"You don't go gray or anything though, right?"

"Not for thousands of years, if even then," he says. "So what else?"

"The second session was about vampire rules and regs. Basically don't ever tell anyone what you are and don't convert anyone without asking first. Oh, and don't use your new powers in any way to attract attention."

Uncle Mortie snorts. "That's a crock. I know of at least three pro NFL players and a couple of NBA guys that are vampires. Don't tell me they aren't putting their power to good use."

I figure this is a good time to delve into Uncle Mortie's shady past. No Mom or Dad around to steer the conversation in a safe direction.

"You weren't exactly a normal conversion though, right?"

Uncle Mortie laughs. "There's nothing normal about me, Mina my girl. I drove those fuss-budget Council members batty as soon as they got wind of me." He takes an exit into a part of downtown I've never been in. A kind of shady neighborhood, if by "shady" you mean dark, dismal, and deserted. Just the kind of place you'd figure Uncle Mortie would hang out in.

"So what happened exactly? I've only ever gotten the way-edited version from Dad."

He looks over at me with what passes for a serious expression for Uncle Mortie. I try to ignore the fact that he's still driving even though he isn't even remotely looking at the road and keep a polite but interested look on my face. He finally turns back to the road. I remember to breathe again.

"Well, I suppose you're old enough to hear the real story now. But we're almost there. Remind me later and I'll tell you the whole sordid thing."

"Deal." I just *know* there has to be more to the story than what I've been able to piece together.

Uncle Mortie parks the car next to a rundown warehouse-type building. Other than a few beat-up cars, and a stray pigeon, there's nothing around.

"Where exactly are we?" This is exactly the kind of place Dad is always telling me *not* to go.

"We're going to a blood bar. They're hosting a turning tonight and I thought you'd be interested in seeing it. It's an open one. Some people like to do it privately, but a lot of folks hold open ones and it's like a big party."

I look around the empty street with the overflowing dumpsters, missing street signs, and broken down buildings. Lovely. "The blood bar is here?"

Uncle Mortie looks around like he's seeing the neighborhood for the first time. I guess my tone of voice tipped him off that I wasn't exactly wowed by the scenery. "Yeah. They aren't all in locations like this, you know. I guess this neighborhood is a little seedier than most. But it's very safe. No one comes here, so you don't have to worry about anything."

No wonder. I wouldn't come here either.

He leads me to a side door on the big warehouse place. An ancient-looking sign above the door says, Harker Brothers Supply Company.

"Funny," I say.

"What?" Uncle Mortie looks up and down the block like he's looking for a clown on a unicycle or something.

"Harker Brothers," I say, pointing to the sign. "You know, Jonathan Harker?"

"Never heard of him."

"From *Dracula*." Does nobody read anymore? Sheesh.

"Oh," says Uncle Mortie. "Never read it. But I do love that Bela Lugosi." He knocks three times on the door. After a few minutes of utter silence, the door creaks open. No one is standing there, but

Uncle Mortie just walks right in, so I follow him. The door closes behind us all by itself.

It's still eerily quiet and the inside of the place doesn't look much better than the outside. Cobwebs everywhere and the only light (from one bare bulb hanging on by a string above the door) is dim at best. And I still can't hear anything or anyone.

"They could totally hold a horror movie here," I whisper to Uncle Mortie.

He laughs and it sounds particularly loud in the small space. "C'mon," he chuckles, "it's not that bad. Just wait until we're in the bar itself. It's up this way."

He leads me up a flight of stairs, down a long hall, up another flight of stairs and to a huge metal door. I guess they don't have any such thing as handicap accessible laws in the vampire world. Hmmm. But I guess there wouldn't be any handicapped vampires, would there? What with all the body changes and things? I don't know.

Uncle Mortie presses a button next to the big metal door and waves to a surveillance camera installed just above it. "My niece," he mouths to the camera. The door opens excruciatingly slowly. The wider it opens the more strange noises and smells assault me. Once the opening is wide enough to fit through, Uncle Mortie pulls me through.

We stop just inside and the door closes behind us. There's

pretty much just one mammoth room and it is absolutely packed with people. I mean, vampires. Whatever. It's almost as dimly lit as the rest of the building, but in a much more artsy-fartsy way with these cool-looking blown glass lights in all different colors. I can barely see to the other side of the room.

"You can close your mouth," Uncle Mortie jokes. "I don't think there're any flies in here, but you never know." I snap my mouth shut. I hadn't even realized it was open.

He leads me through the crowd to a bar on one wall that runs almost the entire length of the place and amazingly, finds two empty seats for us to sit on. Dad's always saying that Uncle Mortie is a partying pro. I can see what he means now.

"What'll you have?" A bartender—or a bloodtender?—suddenly appears in front of us.

"I'll have an O negative, straight up," says Uncle Mortie. The bartender looks at me next.

Oh God.

I am not prepared to drink blood at this time. No way. No how. I don't care if you're supposed to do as Romans do in Rome or whatever. There is no way I'm touching blood. I think I'm going to throw up.

Uncle Mortie takes pity on me and jumps in. "My niece'll have a regular lemonade, please. She's a new prospect."

"Sure thing," says the bartender and disappears to go do whatever you do to make drinks at a blood bar.

I start breathing again.

"They carry normal stuff too. And mixers. A lot of first-timers start off with a blood and Coke or a real Bloody Mary. The really authentic places actually guarantee the blood is from a Mary."

I start turning green.

"But, uh, don't think about any of that right now," says Uncle Mortie, like I'll ever be able to get the image out of my head. I may never drink Coke again. "It's not good for you until you turn. Humans can get sick off of blood."

Yep. Like me. Right now.

"Bathroom." I manage to croak out.

Uncle Mortie points to the opposite side of the room. "I'll just wait here for you, okay?" I nod and dart in the direction he pointed.

Luckily, the bathrooms turn out to be the only well-lit area in the place. And whoo-hoo! No line. I dash inside and duck into a stall, breathing a little heavy.

I don't actually throw up, but it does take me a good five minutes to calm my stomach down. I try to think of as many boring non-food-related things as I can but I keep coming back to my big dilemma.

Am I crazy to be even considering turning? What if I wound

up starving because I couldn't bring myself to drink blood? Like some kind of anorexic vampire or something. How sick would that be? Literally. I finally push out of the stall and splash some water on my face.

"You're not looking too good, kid."

I jump like at least a mile in the air. This vampire lady in a slinky black dress and stiletto heels is next to me putting on lipstick. Blood red, of course. I didn't hear her come in at all.

"First time?" she asks sympathetically.

I nod, not quite trusting myself to speak yet.

"I remember my first time in a blood bar," she says, looking off somewhere into the distance. "It was exciting. Stimulating. All the beautiful vampires dancing to weird and wonderful music, drinking strange concoctions, exotic smells floating in the air." She looks back at me, a little wistfully. "And also completely gross, right?"

I nod again and try to smile at her.

"Don't worry." She pats my arm with a well-manicured hand. "It gets better. And once you turn, you never look back."

"Is it worth it?" I ask her. Somehow, it feels easier to ask a stranger.

She thinks a minute, reapplying the lipstick. "Yes," she says finally, so softly I can barely hear her. "It is. But it isn't for everyone." She puts a hand on either side of my face and looks deep into my eyes, as intense as G.W. but not nearly as threatening. "You think about it long and hard and don't let anyone talk you into anything either way. It's your choice. My boyfriend pressured me into it and I'm glad I did it now, but I didn't do it for the right reasons back then."

"What are the right reasons?" Could someone, anyone, give me a clue here?

She drops her hands and turns back to the mirror. "Everyone's reasons are different. What's right for me wouldn't be right for you. You'll have to figure that out on your own, I'm afraid. But I can tell you that doing it or not doing it to please someone else is the wrong reason."

Ugh. I knew she was going to say something like that. Something all afterschool special.

"Good luck," she says and walks out the door. I give it a second or two, take a deep breath, and then leave the bathroom. No sign of the woman at all. These vampires have a serious disappearing habit. Or talent, I guess.

On my way back to Uncle Mortie and the bar, someone grabs my elbow and swings me around. I nearly freak before I realize that it's Aubrey. And Raven right behind him. Seeing him makes my heart skip a beat, even with Raven there with him. How can he hang out with her?

"Mina," yells Aubrey over the music. "I didn't know you were coming tonight." He gives me one of his flashbulb smiles.

"Me either," I yell back. "My uncle surprised me."

"Nice," he says and waves to Raven. "You know Raven, right? She told me about the turning. It sounds like it will be really cool. I can't wait to see it."

I nod and give a little wave to Raven, just to be polite. She doesn't bother to do anything in return. She's obviously not real happy that I'm here or that Aubrey noticed me.

"Aubrey, we should find some seats. We don't want to miss anything. I see two right over there." Raven points to a spot over by the center of the room where there's a raised platform. I don't see any open seats, but I do note how she mentioned two seats and not three. I can tell when I'm not wanted.

"I'm over at the bar with my uncle," I say to Aubrey, ignoring Raven completely. Two can play that game.

"I haven't been to the bar yet," says Aubrey, but before he can get anything else out, Raven literally grabs him by the arm and drags him off toward the spot she'd pointed to before. I give him a little wave. I'm certainly not going to follow after him like a little lost kitten. He waves back, a little confused. Maybe he's not used to the cave girl approach that Raven seems to like.

I go on back to Uncle Mortie. "Who were those two?" he asks. What they say about vampire eyesight must be true. I don't know how he could have seen us through the crowd or the fake smoke that had started pouring out of the ceiling.

"Two of the kids from the vampire sessions. Aubrey, the guy? He's coming over for dinner tomorrow."

"Oh, is he now," says Uncle Mortie. "Handsome fellow. If you like that sort of thing."

I didn't bother to ask him what he meant by that. I could imagine. If Uncle Mortie had been born a woman, he'd be into the muscle-bound jock type. I just know it. I sip the lemonade waiting on the bar for me. Not bad and thankfully, not pink either.

People-watching in this place is a hoot. There are all types of vampires milling around, dancing, drinking, laughing, and having a good time. Some are dressed in regular clothes; others have on get ups ranging from sixteenth- century haute couture to stuff that could easily belong on the set of a Star Wars movie. I don't see any-body else as pretty as the woman I ran into in the bathroom, but they all look healthy and almost, I dunno, shiny. Like if you saw just one of them in a group of regular people, you'd definitely notice them. It's harder to pick anyone out here when they're all over. It makes me wonder just how bad Uncle Mortie looked *before* he turned.

"Done with your lemonade?" I avoided looking at Uncle Mortie until he downed his O negative. Didn't think my stomach could take it.

"Sure," I say. "What's next?"

"This way," says Uncle Mortie, and takes my hand to pull me through the crowd gathering around the stage area. "I had a buddy of mine save us some good seats."

He pulls me right past Raven and Aubrey, who are seated in the low-rent section. I give them a little finger wave and giggle as we swoop right on by there and go right to a reserved area just off the stage. Thank you, Uncle Mortie, and take that, Goth Girl. I bet Aubrey wishes he'd ditched her for me now.

It's wall-to-wall vampires, all gathered around the stage. I don't know what the signal was. Maybe there's some kind of sixth sense that vampires have for when the party's about to get started. That would explain a lot about Uncle Mortie.

After a minute or two, the whole crowd goes silent as two guys come up on the stage. The nervous-looking one is obviously the new convert. He's an average-looking surfer dude with blond hair and a California tan. The vampire guy is much more impressive, with a wild mane of pitch-black hair and an outfit that would put any of the current crop of boy bands to shame.

Wild Man takes center stage and holds up his hands. "Thank you all for coming out tonight to welcome Scott into the fold." The crowd erupts into a cheering, clapping mob. Shouts of "Welcome, Scott!" ring out. Scott looks almost embarrassed by the

111

enthusiasm, but he smiles a little and gives a bit of a wave. The cheers finally die down when Wild Man lowers his hands and turns to face Scott.

"Scott, do you knowingly and willingly choose to accept the gift you are about to receive?"

Scott freezes for a moment, like a guy caught peeking into the girl's locker room. He looks out at the crowd as if searching for an answer. Everyone is dead silent, but you can almost feel something in the air. They want him to turn and be one of them. But you also don't get the feeling they'd turn on him if he didn't. It's more of a good vibe than anything else. I hold my breath waiting to see what he'll do.

Scott finally turns to stare directly into Wild Man's eyes. "Yes," he says softly, "I do."

No one cheers or anything this time, but you can practically sense the sigh of relief. I'll have to ask Uncle Mortie later what would have happened if he'd said no. Would they just let you go? Do you become dinner? What?

A robed and hooded figure (Geez, these people have seen too many horror movies or something) comes on stage and hands Wild Man a golden goblet encrusted with jewels. I'm no expert or anything, but they look real to me. That thing must be worth thousands. And it looks ancient.

Wild Man takes the goblet in one hand and holds his other just above it. Before I have any idea of what's going on and can prepare myself, the hooded vampire pulls out an antique knife and slices Wild Man's wrist open. I jump in my seat and Uncle Mortie takes my hand. I hear a gasp behind me that sounds suspiciously like Goth Girl.

Blood slowly drains from Wild Man's slashed wrist into the goblet. I can't look away from it and neither can Scott. It's mesmerizing the way it steadily drips, drips, drips. The wound begins closing up and the cut is healed completely by the time the goblet is about half full.

I feel like I should be totally grossed out, but I'm not. I don't know why. Maybe it's the whole solemn ceremony feel or the subtle encouragement I can feel emanating from the vampires around me, but I'm not nearly as freaked out as I think I should be. Uncle Mortie squeezes my hand.

Wild Man hands the goblet to Scott, whose hands are noticeably shaking. He slowly raises the goblet to his lips, hesitates a moment more, and then tosses the whole thing back like he just wants to get it over with. Meanwhile, more hooded figures have brought an ornate carved chair out and placed it on the stage just behind Scott. They gently push him down into the chair and he closes his eyes.

The crowd starts a low chant of "Scott, Scott, Scott," which you'd think would come across like people cheering for a basketball player or something, but it doesn't. With the dim lighting and remnants of smoke swirling around, it's almost like a dark cocoon has covered the whole room. The whole place feels like liquid around me. I shiver a little and Uncle Mortie squeezes my hand again. I'm glad he's here with me, even though it is Uncle Mortie.

Scott suddenly throws his head back and I nearly jump out of my seat again. Good thing Uncle Mortie has a death grip on my hand. The chanting seems to swell around us. Scott looks like he's blurring around the edges, but he doesn't seem to be in any pain. At least, he's not screaming or anything.

The blurriness fades away and suddenly he seems crisper than before. More there. His muscles are more defined and his eyes, when he opens them, are now a startling pure blue. His California tan has faded to a mere memory. He smiles at everyone and stands up and the crowd goes absolutely wild again. Vampires start pouring on to the stage to hug him and shake his hand.

"That's it?" I ask Uncle Mortie.

"Pretty much. He'll be experiencing a lot of internal changes over the next few weeks, but he's officially a vampire now," he says. "What did you expect?"

I don't know what I expected. I guess from movies and books I thought that there'd be bone-crunching pain or something like that. Or you had to seriously kill yourself or something. Or someone was supposed to bite you, rather than you drinking their blood. "I dunno. I guess . . . I mean, well, I guess that wasn't so bad." Aside from the whole slashing the wrist open thing.

"Nah," says Uncle Mortie. "Not bad at all. It actually feels kind of good, like a rush of adrenaline."

"But what about the whole biting thing? Isn't that how you turned Dad?"

"Yeah, though it's actually very rare to get turned that way. Some of your blood has to mix with your victim's blood or be ingested by them. Biting by itself won't turn anyone." He looks at me as seriously as I've ever seen him look. "I'm not proud of what happened with your dad. I didn't mean to turn him. I just really didn't know what I was doing at all during that time. I want you to know that I regret the impact this has had on all your lives."

I pat Uncle Mortie on the hand at a complete loss for words. I'm not used to him going all soul-searching on me. My earlier question occurs to me and I change the subject. "What would have happened if that Scott guy decided not to go through with it?"

Uncle Mortie looks around at the crowd still flowing around us. "We'll talk about that some other time," he says. "This isn't the best place for that discussion."

Ah. Maybe you do become dinner.

WHY I WOULD MAKE A SUCKY VAMPIRE

1. Since the thought of blood gags me, I'd probably be the world's first anorexic (or would that be bulimic?) vampire. And the only thing worse than drinking blood? Puking it up.

2. I like to sleep.

3. And, I like the beach. Sure, you can still go, but it's not the same when you have to worry about frying your eyes and getting a wicked nasty sunburn.

4. I'm nowhere near cool enough. One thing all those vampires at the blood bar (other than Uncle Mortie, but that's a given) had in common is that they all seemed like total A-list types.

5. I can be a total klutz sometimes. What happens when you combine that with super strength? I'm guessing holes in the wall.

6. I don't exactly have the best handle on my temper, as my mom likes to point out. And there's all this anti-vampire propaganda out there (like that stupid Stoker!). I'm sure The Council wouldn't like it when I kick someone's ass for insulting bloodsuckers, but it would be bound to happen. Some new stupid vampire movie or TV show comes out like every year.

11

MYTH: Vampires have hairy palms.

TRUTH: I . . . ugh. I don't even want to think about that. NOT true.

1:03 A.M.

SereneOne: Mina, r u up?

SereneOne: Helllooooooooo

SereneOne: u theeeeeeeerrrreeeeee???????

SereneOne: Mina, Mina, bo-bean-a

MinaMonster: ok ok i'm up! u happy? I gotta rmember to log off this thing b4 i go 2 sleep

SereneOne: srry to wake u, i know u need that beauty sleep...but tonite was soooo sweeeettt!

MinaMonster: nice lol

SereneOne: srry u missed it, but it was sooo awesome. u have an ok time with Mortie?

MinaMonster: not too bad. but tell me bout u—wht happened?

SereneOne: bore city at first. no one wuld get in the pool n i didnt know enyl enuff to talk to em. but then Nathan 'accidentally' knocked Bethany in...

MinaMonster: no way!!! lol!!

SereneOne: yah, knew u'd luv that

MinaMonster: i'd pay major $$$$ to c tht!

SereneOne: then everybody was jumpin in n out and it was hot. nd did i mention Nathan's house is friggin humungo???. he like has his own living room

MinaMonster: jealous much?

SereneOne: an i did talk to Chris sum

MinaMonster: and?? and??

SereneOne: eh, nm. think he's datin that Lisa chickk. the 1 that plays hockey...

MinaMonster: omg

SereneOne: yah, anyway, u go back to sleep. c yah monday

MinaMonster: Nighty-night

Sunday morning was a complete waste. I spent the whole time checking my hair, checking my outfit, checking to make sure Mom wasn't going to cook anything gross, cleaning my room (like Aubrey's even going to see it, but hey, who knows), and acting like a total freak.

118

"Good heavens," Mom said, after I'd asked her for the third time what she was making for dinner (pork chops, green beans, and mashed potatoes with pineapple upside-down cake for dessert— yum). "You're acting like you've never even seen a boy before. Calm down!"

So here I sit in my room. My sparkling clean room. I don't even recognize it. I even hid Mr. Lumps, my old teddy bear, in the closet. Mom is right. I need to get a grip. After all, he's just a boy.

A really, really, really hot boy.

Coming to my house. For dinner.

I change clothes (again) into a short denim skirt and a sexy light blue camisole. Too blue. I try a pair of khakis and a button-down shirt. Too prep. Five outfits later and I'm back where I started in a pair of jeans and a nice top. Oh well. He'd better like the real me.

I sit down at my desk and pull out a sheet of college rule paper. (I hate wide rule. It's too big. I only use it when I have to write a certain number of pages in Ms. Tweeter's class. That's a trick that I learned from Tim Mathis, so I guess he is good for something.) Is it crazy that I even babble in my own mind? Oh man, I hope not. I'd be certifiable.

All in all, this has been a memorable weekend. First Nathan, then the whole turning ceremony thing, and now Aubrey over for dinner. I'm not sure which thing I'm most psyched about.

On the one hand, I've known Nathan for years and have been totally lusting after him for pretty much all that time. Except for that one summer I spent dreaming about Vin Diesel. But that's another story. He's totally cute in a preppy, jock-ish sort of way. Nathan, that is. Not Vin Diesel.

But Aubrey . . . Aubrey is hot in like a movie star kind of way. Like Brad Pitt before he got all stubbly and cut his hair short. Or Ashton, if he wasn't all over Demi Moore. I mean, what's up with that anyway? Cradle robber. And just to be fair, Harrison Ford and that Calista Flockhart totally gross me out too. Keep within your age group, people!

Anyway. Aubrey has this whole older man feel. I know he's the same age, but he's just kind of worldly. Nathan's more like the boy next door.

I can't believe I'm sitting here debating the relative merits of two really hot guys, either of which would trump every other guy I've ever dated. By far. Me, Mina Hamilton, who hasn't had a real date since second quarter with that guy Serena set me up with. It was a total flop. He was addicted to one of those online role-playing things and all he could talk about was his hit points and armor rating.

Another plus for both Nathan and Aubrey. They don't seem like the type to be addicted to a computer game.

So, my list so far:

NATHAN	AUBREY
* Have liked since forever	* Just met
* Adorable	* Hunky
* Preppy, but hot	* Sexy fashion sense
* Total puppy dog eyes	* Intense green eyes
* Can't tell him anything about the vampire thing. Isn't his dad like a judge or something?	* Knows about the whole vampire thing and is, of course, okay with it as he wants to be one
* No idea on Nathan's family stance. But he's been nice to everyone else	* Seems to like my parents, not that they've met yet. So, family-oriented
* Knows Serena and is nice to her	* He puts up with Raven, so Serena should be a shoe-in
* Not addicted to computer games	* Not addicted to computer games
* Invited us to pizza and even saved seats	* Invited himself over for dinner
* Totally dissed Bethany	* Would probably diss Bethany. I would hope
* Considerate	* Takes charge

Other than the vampire thing, they seem to match up fairly
evenly. But that one thing does make a big difference. If I decide

121

to turn, it's not like I could keep going out with Nathan. I mean, if he's truly interested. He seems to be. Or could I swing it? Have to ask Mom how that whole dating-another-species thing works. I guess it's like another species. Or race maybe? I don't know if there's really a good scientific term for it. I mean, you can't breed anymore . . . though breeding makes it sound so, I don't know, clinical.

Thankfully, the doorbell rings and I stop that train of thought to leap up, bonk my knee on the desk, and sprint to the front door before anyone else can get there. I take a deep breath, paste what I hope is a sexy, intriguing, New-Me smile on, and open the door.

"Hey, Mina," says Uncle Mortie, handing me a casserole dish. "Thought I'd invite myself over for dinner so I can check out this guy." He looks me up and down. "You have a toothache or something?"

Oh great. As if one overprotective male relative wasn't bad enough. And I guess I need to work on my sexy smile.

"Mortie?" Mom calls from the kitchen. "Is that you? I didn't know you were coming over." She comes out into the hall. "I'm not sure I have enough pork chops to go around." Yes! Go home, Uncle Mortie!

"Never fear, my dear, I brought my famous casserole to share."

I hand Mom the casserole dish. She takes it and tries to hide her grimace of utter horror. Uncle Mortie's casserole is famous all right, but not in the way you'd want. I think it's the only thing he can cook, if you can call what he does to unsuspecting food cooking. It's supposed to be a tuna-salmon-cheese-bacon-noodle-rice-potato-surprise, but it pretty much just comes out like congealed leftovers that were left out on the counter too long and then refrozen.

"How nice," says Mom gamely. "We'll just, uh, reheat it." She hands it back to me and whispers "Put it in the oven at 450."

I head to the kitchen while Mom and Uncle Mortie chat it up. Four hundred fifty degrees sounds a little high to me, but what do I know? I'm a better cook than Uncle Mortie, but I'm not exactly Martha Stewart or anything.

The doorbell rings again and I almost drop the casserole dish as I'm popping it in the oven, which would have solved that problem. I do a fast walk (can't be seen running to the door now, since Mom's probably already answered it) and find Aubrey shaking hands with Uncle Mortie and Mom holding a bouquet of flowers. How nice is that? I can't believe he brought me flowers! Nathan is going to have to work a little harder . . .

"Hi, Aubrey," I say, slowing down my fast walk to a saunter. Don't want him to think I'm too anxious.

"Hi, Mina." He smiles one of those mouthwatering smiles at

me and I melt a little inside. "I was just telling your mother how much I appreciate her letting me come over for dinner."

So, he's a bit of a suck up. That's okay. Certainly can't hurt as far as parent points go. Uncle Mortie shoots me a bemused look. I can only imagine what he's thinking. I bet he's never sucked up to anyone in his life. Lied to them, yeah.

"I'll just go put these in some water," Mom says. "Mina, why don't you give Aubrey the grand tour?" In other words, stay out of my hair while I try to find another pork chop for Uncle Mortie, but make sure you don't stay in any one room too long or I'll have to go check on you.

So I give Aubrey the "grand'" tour, which is really not all that grand. Our place is okay, but it isn't anything to write home about. Does that make sense? How could you write home ... about home? Anyway, I dutifully lead him around, pointing out the highlights. You know, here's a picture of me when I was a cute little kid. Here's Dad's bowling trophy. Yeah, I know, I can't believe he bowls either. Yep, my mother knits, don't sit on that afghan, she's not done with it yet. And here's my room, cleaner than it has ever been in the entire history of me having a room.

Aubrey ooohs and aaahs in all the appropriate places, periodically asking questions about how long we've lived here (since I was like seven or so), what Mom and Dad do for a living (middle-school teacher and accountant, respectively), do I have any brothers or sisters (nope), do they do any work for The Council (have no idea, but I sincerely doubt it). We end up in the kitchen where an absolutely horrific burning smell is coming from the oven. Uncle Mortie's casserole! Aubrey's wrinkling his nose as politely as he can and I rush to the oven to take it out, but Mom waves me away. "I've got it," she whispers. "Go ahead and take Aubrey to the dining room." In a louder voice she calls out, "Oh no, Mortie, it looks like I've ruined your casserole!"

I've got to hand it to Mom. She's sneaky. She's a good woman to have on your side.

I lead Aubrey on to the dining room and he very diplomatically says nothing about the scene in the kitchen or the rank smell of burned casserole we happily leave behind. It's amazing. I'm not nearly that polite. Or reserved. I'd have been all over that, if I were in his shoes. So I feel the need to clarify it a little, so he doesn't think we're too weird. As if.

"Uncle Mortie can't cook," I explain. "But he brought the casserole over anyway. Mom was just saving us from having to actually eat it."

"I see," says Aubrey, smiling courteously. I swear, this guy is unflappable. I get a sudden urge to poke him in the ribs to see what he'd do, but I restrain myself successfully.

I rack my brain to come up with a good topic to discuss that will last longer than two sentences—me saying something and Aubrey agreeing. "So, what did you think of the turning ceremony the other night?"

He finally gets a little animated. "Oh, it was great! I'm really glad I got to see it. I didn't know they made such a ritual out of it. In *Blood Always Drips Down* there was a turning, but Brighton only had his sister there to witness it. I can't wait to have my own ceremony. I know just where to have it and what I'm going to wear."

Whoa. That's so . . . girly. I haven't even figured out what I'm going to wear to prom yet (provided I actually get to go), and I'm the female here. It suddenly occurs to me that this incredibly handsome guy just might be gay. Wouldn't that just be my luck? My old luck. It's like my mom's best friend says, all the good ones are either taken or gay. Or both.

But then why would he have invited himself over for dinner?

"You have anyone special coming to your ceremony?" Okay, not the smoothest way to ask, but it was all I could come up with on short notice and I've got to know. Is he gay? Not that I have anything against gay people at all. I don't. I just don't want to get hung up on one. I'm not one of those self-inflated girls who think they can get a gay guy to switch party lines. I mean, you bat for whichever team you bat for. Well, unless you play for both teams.

Whatever. I'm getting bogged down in sports clichés.

"Not really," he says, which doesn't help at all. "I don't really talk to my family much. We don't have much in common. And I couldn't really tell them anyway. I wasn't lucky enough to have vampires in the family like you. Everything I've learned about vampires has come from books and the vampire sessions. But I've done a lot of research."

Grrr. Polite and vague. Perfect.

"Lucky, huh?" Uncle Mortie comes in from the living room and sits down. So much for time alone with the (possibly gay) love of my life.

"I've wanted to be a vampire ever since I can remember," says Aubrey. "It's all I've ever wanted. I read everything I could get my hands on about it. And I watch all the movies too, of course. But I'm not sure if you can really trust Hollywood about anything important. I'd trust Melman over some director any day. Brighton Powell is my hero."

"Hmmmm," says Uncle Mortie.

Dad comes in and saves us from anymore grilling. He shakes hands with Aubrey and they start chatting about some football team or something. That's a good sign. Most of the gay guys I know aren't really into sports. Well, not normal guy-sports like football and basketball. More like swim team or figure skating.

Things like that. Though I suppose there are gay guys who watch football. I mean, hey, big buff guys in tight pants. What's not to like there? I know that's why I'd watch it.

Mom sweeps into the room carrying a platter of pork chops and gives me a nod, my cue to go get the side dishes. We all settle in for dinner and there's little talking going on for the first few minutes as we stuff down food. Politely, of course. As nervous as I have been all day, I'm happy to be getting anything down and even happier that I haven't spilled anything (yet).

"So," says Dad to Aubrey, "We hear you're in the vampire sessions with Mina. How do you like them so far?"

"They aren't too bad, but we don't get to spend much time with actual vampires to get a feel for what's really going on. Other than Ms. Riley."

"What about your sponsor? Who do you have?"

"Bradley Sloan. But he's on The Council, so I haven't been able to get much time with him. He's a busy man."

I can tell from the sour look that Dad and Mom share that they aren't big fans of Mr. Sloan.

Aubrey doesn't notice. "That's why I was so happy to find out that Mina's family is all vampires." He smiles at me and I bask in the glow for a minute. "Thank you again for letting me come over for dinner."

"How did you get mixed up with Bradley Sloan?" asks Uncle Mortie. Another non-Sloan fan, by the tone of his voice. I should check out this guy. What is that old cliché? Something about keeping your enemies close. Maybe he's the reason why it's suddenly so important for me to decide the entire rest of my life in just a month. The jerk!

"As I was telling Mina, I've wanted to be a vampire all my life. Or, at least for so long that I can't even remember when I didn't want to be one. I spent years researching everything I could find. There's a lot of information out there, if you dig deep enough. Anyway, I figured out that Bradley was a vampire and I approached him last year. He agreed to sponsor me."

"Hmmmm," says Uncle Mortie again.

Hmmmm indeed. What about G.W. and the whole keeping things a secret? I guess members of The Council don't necessarily follow their own rules.

"Interesting," says Dad.

The rest of the night was pretty much Aubrey asking questions about stuff that would never have occurred to me to ask. Mom, Dad, and Uncle Mortie took turns answering him. I didn't really get another word in the entire night. I haven't been on tons of dates, but this by far was the most boring date I have ever been on, even if Aubrey was a pleasure to look at. So I occupied myself with cataloging his best features and comparing him to various actors. He nearly always came out on top, except for his ears. They were okay ears, but a little bit pointy.

The highlight was when Mom gave Aubrey a shorter version of the sex talk we'd had and Dad turned three different shades of purple. That was worth sitting through all the rest to see. Aubrey just hung on every word like it was the gospel and he'd seen the light.

It wasn't until he was getting ready to leave that I got a chance to speak with him alone again. It was my last chance to figure out if he was gay or not. None of the Q&A sessions had pointed either way, darn it.

"So," I say, "hope you had a good time."

"Great! Thank you again for having me over. I think I learned a lot."

Grrr. Not exactly what I was going for. Dates aren't supposed to be enlightening. They're supposed to be fun. Sexy. Crazy. I decide to take the plunge and just pop the big question.

"Do you have a girlfriend?"

Okay, so I kind of chickened out. I could have said "significant other" but I went the safe route instead. If he's not gay, I really don't want to imply that he is. Guys tend to be real touchy about that.

He looks a little taken aback, but answers with his usual politeness. "No. Honestly, between my research and the whole turning process, I haven't had time. And it wouldn't be fair to start a relationship up with a human anyway."

"Right, exactly," I say. "I know just what you mean." But I don't, really. He said "human," not "girl" or even "boy." So I'm back at square one with my burning question.

"See you on Tuesday." He gives me a quick hug (A hug? What's up with that?) and just takes off. No lip action. Well, that was a total waste. Either he's gay or just not interested. Maybe because I'm not a vampire? But I'm thinking about it. That should count for something.

I go back inside and narrowly miss stepping on Uncle Mortie, who must have been spying on me from the peephole. Not that there was anything to see.

"Nice enough kid," says Uncle Mortie, backpedaling into the living room, but not looking the least bit guilty. "But you could do better."

"No one is good enough for my baby," says Dad from the kitchen, where he's helping Mom wash dishes. I snort. He would say that. I could bring home a Nobel Peace Prize winner and he'd probably say the same thing. He's such a dad.

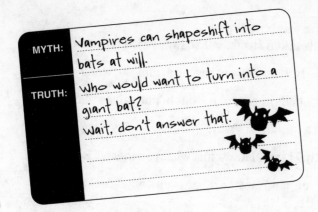

MYTH: Vampires can shapeshift into bats at will.

TRUTH: who would want to turn into a giant bat? wait, don't answer that.

12

I wake up to my cell phone ringing. Who in the world would call me before school? Before my shower and cup of coffee? I pick it up before Mom or Dad comes into the room to turn it off. They finally got me a cell for my sixteenth birthday after essentially being locked out of using the home phone since I discovered it at twelve. Hey, what can I say? I am a teenager.

"Hello?"

"Girl, you forgot to call me *again!*" It's Lorelai. That is one determined cheerleader when it comes to snooping into other people's relationships.

"Sorry about that. I completely forgot. But honestly, not a whole lot to report. He chatted up the 'rents the whole time he was here."

"Huh."

Did I make it sound worse than it was? "He did bring flowers." I neglect to mention that he gave them to my mom.

"Okay, well, that's something. But he's definitely behaving very borderline."

Does she suspect that he's gay too? Is it obvious to everyone but me? And Raven, I guess. "Borderline?"

"At this stage in a relationship," explains Lorelai patiently, as if I'm only twelve and had just started dating (only partly true, since I have been on *some* dates but I'm way past twelve), "he should be showering you with attention. Sucking up to parents isn't until at least stage five. Technically, he shouldn't even have met them yet."

"Ah." I wonder how many stages there are. I'd ask, but I don't want her to think I'm totally clueless.

"I'll scope him out for you on Tuesday. See if I can learn anything. Maybe he's just a slow bloomer. Or he could be attached . . . "

"He said he didn't have a girlfriend."

She snorts into the phone. "I've known guys to lie."

"True." And I bet she has too. Cute, perky vampire-wannabe cheerleader. It's a given.

"I've got to get to school. I'll see ya on Tuesday."

"Sure. Thanks. For the checking up thing. And all. Bye!" I guess I'll forgive her for the early morning wake-up call. After all, I could definitely use her cheerleader-guy know-how.

133

You know, I don't think that I've really ever been in a good stage-one relationship, much less stage five. I don't know that I've ever been absolutely showered with attention. Bobby Wilson did give me flowers that one time, but I'm pretty sure it was his mom's idea.

I drag myself out of bed and get ready for school. I'd already given Serena the scoop on the Aubrey dinner fiasco last night (I did remember to call her), so our morning ride was pretty quiet. Mondays are usually low-key days for both of us. Serena even has a CD of Monday music that she plays at the start of every week. It's got songs like Bob Geldof's "I Hate Mondays." I didn't even know he sang. He's like some kind of activist guy now, but I guess he was big in the 80s.

Even the teachers seem to have the Monday blues today. Madame Tilly just gives us some French poetry to read (soppy love stuff, at least as far as I can tell) and Mr. Jackson only yells at someone once (he normally blows up at least five times) in Chemistry when Tim sets something on fire. And I can totally see why he'd yell then.

George stops by at lunch. I offer him a seat and officially introduce him to Serena. He's pretty chipper. I guess he doesn't have any existential problems to deal with, like wondering whether the potential love of your life is gay.

"How'd you like the basket weaving?" Serena asks him.

He looks blankly at her, which is hardly surprising since I hadn't mentioned the change in lectures to him.

"It was like the history of basket weaving, actually," I butt in. "We didn't get to make any baskets or anything on Thursday." I kick him under the table.

"Oh, yeah," he says. "Like the different kinds of straw and things like that. Pretty boring."

"Given," says Serena. "I'm glad my parents don't make me go to that kind of stuff."

George gets a little twinkle in his eye and I think, uh-oh. I'm beginning to learn that look. Last time I saw it, he convinced Lorelai that there were cheerleaders in ancient Rome.

"This week should be a little more exciting. I hear Tuesday is going to be on dating rituals of the pygmies. And Thursday should be a real winner: the history of pig farming in the Midwestern states."

I almost choke on my lunch. Where does he come up with this stuff? It's great. I'd put him up against Uncle Mortie any day.

Serena totally buys it. "And I thought Chem was bad. I feel sorry for you guys."

George smiles at me and gives me a sly wink. The dog. I am never playing poker with this guy. He could probably keep a straight face with a hand full of aces. Shoot, knowing him, he'd probably have five aces in his hand, just in case, and a good lie on how they got there, if you caught him at it.

Serena plows through a couple more bites of her salad and steals one of my fries when she thinks I'm not looking. George is telling a story about the time he accidentally shaved off one of his fellow foster kid's eyebrows (just the left one) when she gets a bright idea. I can tell because she suddenly starts tapping her index finger against the table and starts wiggling in her seat. That's her oh-hurry-up-and-finish-your-story-so-I-can-tell-you-what-I-just-thought-of thing. She's too nice to actually interrupt, but George must pick up on it, 'cause he hurries up the end of the story.

"I've got a great idea," says Serena.

"About shaving eyebrows?" asks George.

"No," she says and rolls her eyes at him. "About you." That shuts him up and me too. I lean forward. What's she got up her sleeve? Serena's great ideas generally fall into two categories: something that sounds like a great idea but will wind up getting me in a lot of trouble or something that sounds like a terrible idea, will more than likely get me in trouble, but usually works out in the end.

"Nathan mentioned the other night that we all ought to go out sometime and do something. Well, I was thinking it would be kind of odd for just the three of us to go out. You know, someone would always be the odd man out. So I was thinking George could come with!"

I'm not sure which of the two categories this idea falls under. It sounds like a straightforward enough idea, but somehow, some way, I'm sure there'll be trouble in it for me. But maybe this is just Serena's backhanded way of asking George out. After all, she kind of hinted that she thought he was cute, and that jock guy she was lusting after was a complete dud (big surprise).

So I say, "Sure, whaddaya think, George?"

He looks like a cornered rabbit for a minute, then squares his shoulders and says, "Why not." Heh. Brave man.

"Great," says Serena. "I'll set it up. It'll be fun!"

George looks like he has serious doubts, but then he launches into another story about the time he accidentally glued himself to his desk in the fifth grade and soon we're laughing so hard that I forget to be worried about it.

Serena's got a mind like a steel trap though and she doesn't forget about it at all. She corners Nathan as soon as we get to sixth-period English. I swear, get the girl out of the Goth and next thing you know, she's a regular spitfire.

"So, Nathan," she says, all coy (which works much better in a low-cut T-shirt and jeans than in Goth getup, let me tell you).

"About what you said the other night? About all of us maybe going out and doing something?"

"Yeah?"

"I was thinking maybe this Friday? You, me, Mina, and our friend George?"

"Sure," he says. "Sounds great. I think Jill Mason's having a little get-together. We could check it out and then maybe crash at my place. That work for you guys?" He looks from me to Serena and back again.

"Perfect," we say in unison. He laughs.

"Always together, never apart. It's the Serena-Mina!"

If I'd known how simple it was to get into the in crowd and hang out with Nathan, I'd have tried it years ago. Apparently, all you have to do is ask. Who knew?

Ms. Tweeter interrupts my train of thought as she sweeps into the room. Today she's dressed as a bat, I suppose because of the whole vampires-turning-into-bats thing. Oh, she's batty all right.

But here's the real scoop, which I gathered during vampire lesson number one. Yes, shape-shifting is possible, though not all vampires can manage to do it. However, there's this little thing called matter transference. Something as big as a person can't shape-shift into something as little as a bat. You could shape shift

138

into a huge monster bat, but that's a tad bit conspicuous. And it takes years of practice before you get it right—not that I'm not going to try the bat thing if I turn. Oh, no, I'd much rather try turning into something a bit more furry and less flighty. I weigh about 115 pounds soaking wet, so I figure I could easily shape shift into:

a) A pretty big dog like a German shepherd or a rottweiler and terrorize Mrs. Finch's stupid cat and get it to stop using our lawn as his private litter box, or

b) Some kind of zoo animal and slip into the animal cages at night and check out what really happens in the reptile house, or

c) The school mascot (Jimmy IV, a hulking bulldog with seriously bad breath) and sneak into the boy's locker room. Though I've heard it really smells in there. Like Doritos and gym socks.

So Ms. Tweeter flits and flutters around the room for a while and then settles down to alight upon her desk. Literally. She perches on the end of it like she could take off at any minute. I wonder what Principal Harvey would think if he stepped in the room right now?

"I thought we'd do some reading aloud today," she says in a high-pitched voice. Trying to sound like a bat, I suppose. "Mina,

Nathan, why don't you two start us off? You can get in some practice for your project."

You know, I don't care how batty Ms. Tweeter is. I love that woman.

We both take our books and sit on the stools in the front of the class. Ms. Tweeter doesn't let people just read from their desk. She thinks it makes people pay more attention if you're in front of everyone. Sucks to be you if you happen to have stage fright. Luckily, I can make a fool of myself with no problem, though I hopefully won't do it today in front of Nathan. The key is being committed. If you do it half-assed, then you really look like an idiot. If you're totally committed, you at least come off looking like you meant to do it and no one's the wiser.

Ms. Tweeter pops an ancient, dusty hat with a huge feather on top of my head and puts a fedora on Nathan. To get us in the mood, I guess. Whatever. There goes that not-making-a-fool-out-of-yourself thing right out the window. I look like a total dork in hats. I don't have the right shaped head or something.

"Ok, class," she says brightly, "I'm sure you've noticed by now that the book is told primarily through journal entries and correspondence. It's an epistolary novel. And if you haven't, then you're way behind." She wags her finger at the room in general and a few people laugh. Probably the ones that have

140

no idea what she's talking about. "So, we're going to have Mina read out one of Dr. Seward's journal entries where he's reporting on Mina Harker's condition. Nathan will read one of Jonathan's."

She hands me *Dracula*, open to a page fairly late in the game. I sneak a peek at Nathan in his fedora before I start reading. It figures he'd look cute in a dorky hat.

The passage was marked a bit over halfway through Dr. Seward's entry, right after Van Helsing asks Mina to explain what has happened to her.

I read: "I took the sleeping draught which you had so kindly given me, but for a long time, it did not act. I seemed to become more wakeful, and myriads of horrible fancies began to crowd in upon my mind—all of them connected with death, and vampires; with blood, and pain, and trouble."

Only people in books ever talk like that. I mean, myriad? Come on. Who says stuff like that?

It continues on through the Count coming into visit Mina in her stupor. Meanwhile, Ms. Tweeter is acting out everything, even the Count entering the room as a spooky mist (which is a total fiction. Like the whole turning into a teeny-tiny bat thing, vampires can't just disintegrate themselves and show up as, you know, *weather*). When I get to the part where the Count bites Mina on the neck,

I tense up, just waiting for her to make a move at me. Luckily, she doesn't. I guess it's got to be against some kind of school regulation. Biting students, that is.

"I felt my strength fading away, and I was in a half-swoon. How long this horrible thing lasted I know not, but it seemed that a long time must have passed before he took his foul, awful, sneering mouth away. I saw it drip with fresh blood!"

I know this is a Gothic book and all, but for heaven's sake. A half-swoon? Is that like being half-pregnant? I don't think it's possible.

"Then he spoke to me mockingly, 'And so you, like the others, would play your brains against mine. You would help these men to hunt me and frustrate me in my design! You know now, and they know in part already, and will know in full before long, what it is to cross my path. They should have kept their energies closer to home. Whilst they played wits against me—against me who commanded nations, and intrigued for them, and fought for them, hundreds of years before they were born—I was counter-mining them. And you, their best beloved one, are now to me, flesh of my flesh, blood of my blood, kin of my kin; my bountiful winepress for a while; and shall be later on my companion and my helper."

This is so far from the truth.

a) Vampires have never worked for humans (At least, not in any of the history stuff G.W. told us about, and I'd trust her over some old dead white dude.);

b) They don't plot against humans (I mean, after all, they couldn't exist if there were no humans, since they can't have kids. New vampires have to come from *somewhere*.);

c) They try to *avoid* humans ever knowing what they are. (They aren't going to *monologue* about it.)

I'm kind of annoyed about the whole passage, especially the foul breath thing. (Everyone in my family brushes their teeth at least twice a day, thank you very much.) But I try to keep it out of my voice. Ms. Tweeter finally signals for me to stop and I do so with relief. I can hardly take this antivampire propaganda. Okay, yeah, I'm sure there are vampires out there who do take advantage of humans sometimes (like that one that turned Uncle Mortie), but we're not. I mean, *they're* not all evil and foul smelling and reeking of blood. Some of them are even cute. Look at Aubrey, he's going to be one heck of a hot vampire.

Nathan gets to read the part where Jonathan responds to Mina's attack by the Count. He really gets into it and sounds all torn up and angry by turns. I find myself wishing it really was about me that he was talking about, though I do wish he didn't have to curse vampires and all that. It kind of hurts to hear him say it. What will he think if I go through with it? Not that I could even tell him.

But, man, he's just so adorable. Every girl in the class is hanging on his every word. Ms. Tweeter should just have him read everything. That way, at least the girls in the class would always be paying attention.

Maybe there's a passage in the book where Jonathan and Mina get to declare their love for each other. Hmmmm, that would be a great one for our project.

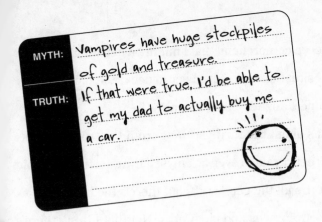

MYTH: Vampires have huge stockpiles of gold and treasure.

TRUTH: If that were true, I'd be able to get my dad to actually buy me a car.

13

George and I are the first ones to arrive at the community center for Tuesday's vampire lesson. They must have had some old folk's event on Monday because the whole place reeks of mothballs and other unidentifiable old people smells. It makes me think of Great-Grandma's nursing home.

That reminds me that poor George has no family to even think about. That's so sad. I can't imagine what it would be like to have no family at all. No one to love you no matter what, nobody to celebrate holidays with. Harsh. I wonder if he's even going to do the ceremony thing when he turns.

"You think you're going to go through with it?" I ask him.

"With what? The whole vampire thing?" I nod. "Yeah," he says. "Why not? Explore the world, live forever. You?"

I don't answer him, but he just continues on without noticing, like he can't even comprehend that I might be debating the issue. "I guess your situation makes it easier to decide. What with your parents and uncle already being vampires."

Huh. That's about the furthest thing from the truth. For me, anyway. I've been afraid to even ask myself the question. It's a big decision. There's all the good stuff, but there's the bad stuff too. Like people with torches and pitchforks. Not that I think there's much danger of that today, but you never know.

"I don't think they'll have a problem with my application. But I'd be worried if I were Raven."

"Why? She looks like a shoe-in. She's got vampire-wannabe written all over her." With emphasis on the wannabe, but I keep that part to myself.

"Exactly. I've heard old G.W. warning her about that. They don't want to advertise or perpetuate those kinds of stereotypes. And Raven . . . I think she just wants to do it for the glamour. Or her idea of glamour, anyway."

"What do they do to you if The Council doesn't approve you?"

"I don't know," says George. "And I don't want to find out."

I'm going to have to corner Uncle Mortie on this one. I need to give him a call. I need to get the scoop on a couple of things from him. If I do decide not to do it, I don't want to end up hamburger or something worse.

"Any idea what's on the agenda today? Other than the dating rituals of pygmies?"

He laughs. "No idea. But I hope it's on something actually useful."

Then he starts in on a story about the time he and another kid ran off to join the circus when he was about ten, not realizing that there aren't very many circuses anymore. They had to go back after they couldn't find one.

"And I really wanted to be a clown too." He finishes. I'm about doubled over with laughter by this time, so I don't even notice Raven, Aubrey, and a few others coming in.

"Looks like you got your wish," Raven sneers. Aubrey and some of the other kids laugh. I can't believe he did that. I shoot a look at all of them. Have I mentioned how I can't stand rude people? They rate right up there with people who cut in line and those jerks that pretend they have injuries so they can get a handicapped sticker.

"Better to be a clown than look like one," I retort back. Not my best effort, but hey. Stress of the moment and all that.

"You say something to me?" Raven walks right up to the chair I'm sitting in and glares down at me. Oh, she so did not want to do that. I stand up, effectively making her get out of the way or get stepped on. I'm a good two or three inches taller than she is, so I look down my nose and right into her beady little kohl-lined eyes.

"Yeah," I say. "And I can think of some other things to say too, but maybe I'll get you a dictionary first so you can understand what I'm saying."

Have I mentioned that I took kickboxing and karate for a few years? I'm not exactly grace under fire, but I've got a heck of a right hook. Just ask Bethany.

Raven looks like she's going to go for it, but then Aubrey steps in.

"Girls, girls," he says. "No need to fight over something so trivial."

I don't think it's trivial. George is a good guy and Raven is a pain in the ass. This isn't the first time she's said something rude to him. Or to me, for that matter. But as soon as Aubrey butts in, Raven simmers right down and makes eyes at him. Gag.

"Oh, you're so right, Aubrey. I don't know what I was thinking." And with that, she leads him away to go chat about, I don't know, the difference between regular eyeliner and kohl.

Aubrey may have the movie-star looks thing going for him, but Nathan is creeping way higher on my list. He'd never act like such a jerk. I sit back down.

"You know," says George, "I can actually take care of myself." He doesn't look mad, though, just more amused than anything else.

I don't know why, but I blush a little. "I'm sure you can. I just can't stand people like that."

"Well, thanks for being willing to beat her up for me. I can't say that I've ever had a girl willing to kick someone's ass for me before."

It's my turn to laugh. "You know it," I say. "Anytime, anywhere. I'm good to go."

"I had no idea you were such a toughie. I'm going to start calling you K-O."

"Ha, ha." That's just what I need, another nickname. And I just finally got people to stop calling me Mona after they misspelled my name freshman year. No one should ever name their kid Mona. I got so many porn jokes thrown at me it wasn't even funny. But the worst nickname I had was in first grade when they called me Meeney-Miney-Mina. Parents should really think of these things before naming their kids. But at least my parents didn't name me Wilhelmina, which was actually the girl's whole name in *Dracula*. Now *that* would have been bad.

Grandma Wolfington comes in followed by three other vampires that I've never seen before. The three of them line up against the wall like toy soldiers at attention. The introduction of the newcomers quiets everybody down fast.

"Good evening, everyone," says G.W. "Tonight we're going to talk about some of the new careers open to you as a vampire. While you can, of course, work in any job a human can, there are also some new options open to you once you turn. I've brought along some guest speakers tonight and I trust you will give them a good reception." She pauses to give us the look of death, a silent warning that we'd better behave or she'll be eating us for breakfast. Perhaps literally.

"Professor McHenry is a historian." The first of the three vampires steps forward and nods to us all. He seems more like an accountant than an Indiana Jones–type, but looks can be deceiving when you're talking about vampires. I'm definitely starting to learn that.

"Vampires have a distinct advantage when compiling histories," he says in a soft voice. "Humans can't interview subjects that were around during the time of the crusades or when the pyramids were built, but we can. But don't let that fool you into thinking this job is easy. A good part of it is tracking down the vampires we need to talk to in exotic and sometimes dangerous locations. Most of what we discover we keep to ourselves—after all, how would we prove the knowledge that we come by to humans?"

Sounds interesting, except for the whole dates and places thing.

History has always bored me to tears. But the traveling thing sounds kind of cool.

Professor McHenry goes on for a while longer about the exciting aspects of history (yeah, right) and a recent trip he took to Borneo to find someone who knew Julius Caesar (okay, that's cool) and then Grandma Wolfington introduces the next vampire.

"Wynnette Samson has a special position, but I'll let her tell you about it."

The second vampire steps smartly forward. A tall, thin woman with slicked back hair and an almost-but-not-quite military-style outfit. She strikes me as someone you wouldn't want to mess with. She strides out to the very middle of the room. She doesn't look at all like a Wynnette.

"You do something wrong"—she booms out—"you deal with me." Everyone shrinks back a little and poor Linda, directly in front of Herr General Samson, looks like she's going to faint.

Herr General proceeds to stomp back and forth across the room. "I am one of a select few elite specialists in vampire law enforcement. I make sure that the laws are followed and if they are not . . . I take care of it." There's no doubt in any of our minds that she would. Painfully. Maybe she's the answer to that question about what happens to new recruits that don't make it. Ouch.

"To become a member of the Vampire Corps, you must be dedicated, responsible, knowledgeable, trustworthy, and above all honorable. You must also go through a rigorous training course designed to weed out the weak among us."

Okay, and obviously, you must also be stark, raving insane. Looking around, I don't think anyone in the room is feeling the love for joining the Corps, except maybe Raven. But I have a sneaking suspicion she might be one of the "weeds" Herr General was talking about.

General Samson goes on barking out information at us for a while longer until Grandma Wolfington interrupts her (I wouldn't have dared) and introduces the last guy.

"Johann Gutter is a member of the Vampire Relocation Agency, or VRA."

This guy steps forward and smiles at us kindly, perhaps to make up for the last speaker. He's an average-looking vampire, probably Swedish or Dutch or something like that.

"Hello everyone," he says in a friendly voice with almost no accent. I suppose even tough accents would disappear after a hundred years or so. Everyone relaxes a little. "I am a vampire relocation specialist. As a VRA agent, my job is to help vampires relocate to a new location with a new identity. We recommend relocation at least every ten years to keep everyone safe, both vampires and humans. Not every move requires a new identity, but we can provide you with everything from a fake death to an entire new life history from scratch."

Interesting. I just figured the disappearing act was something you had to do on your own. This must have been what Mom was talking about. We've been living in our house about ten years now, but we've actually been in town since I was about two or three. So we're officially way overdue for moving. They can't actually make us move, can they? I mean, he did just say that they "recommend" moving every ten years. But do they actually "recommend" it a la General Samson?

He goes on for a while about all of the services they offer and the types of specializations that agents can get into, like counterfeiting or subterfuge. He explains that each vampire's situation is treated as unique and that the service is paid for by a relocation tax.

Oh, yeah. Stupid tax collectors. They're the reason I'm here. Now I understand why adults are always talking about how they hate the tax man.

Grandma Wolfington tells us about a few other careers vampires can look forward to, like being on the Council (blech), teaching at a vampire college (they have their own colleges?), being a human liaison (some kind of human-vampire political thing, something I have *way* too big a mouth for), and performing scientific research into vampirism (also probably not for me, since I almost set my lab partner on fire once).

I wonder why in the world my dad is still an accountant. You'd think he'd have tried something else. He's a big history buff, always watching The History Channel. Or shoot, Mom. Being a middle-school teacher is at least as hazardous as being in the Corps. But I guess all those things take a lot of travel. No wonder most vampires never try to have a family. I bet I've been holding them back all these years.

After the session, George is all excited. "Isn't this cool?"

"What, you going to join the Corps?"

He gives me a look before he figures out I'm joking. "Goof," he says. "I mean some of the other jobs. They all sound pretty cool."

I kind of agree. For once, I feel like I really learned something useful in a session. The new career options do sound more interesting than being an accountant or sitting in a cubicle all day. Especially the ones that involve traveling. I've always wanted to travel. But no way would I want to be in the Corps. That woman was seriously scary.

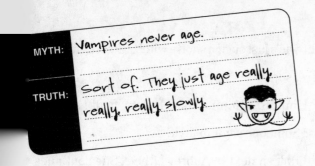

MYTH: Vampires never age.

TRUTH: Sort of. They just age really, really, really slowly.

14

Serena and I have a study date Wednesday night to work on our *Dracula* projects. I'm hanging out in my room waiting for her to come by when the phone rings. I figure she's calling to tell me she's going to be late or something (she's always late, it's her one big fault), so I answer in my best annoying radio announcer voice.

"Well, hello there, little lady!"

But, of course, it isn't Serena. "Uh, Mina?"

"Oh, hey, Lorelai. I thought you were someone else calling." I should really hit my parents up for caller ID and a phone that supports it. At least it wasn't Nathan.

"Girl, you are whacked out. What was that scene between you and Raven yesterday? I didn't get to catch you after the session to get the scoop."

"Nothing much. She's just such a snotty witch. She was ragging on George for no reason."

"George, huh? Hmmm." Hmmm what? Is it my fault I stick up for the underdogs? Someone's got to do it.

"I noticed you didn't sit next to Aubrey either." She continues in an insinuating voice.

"He was over there playing foot solider to Raven. Not the kind of company I keep."

"Uh-huh." Obviously, something is clicking and turning over and over in her little cheerleader head.

"Just spit it out, Lorelai. What're you trying to say?"

"Oh, nothing. I was just wondering if there might be a little Georgey Porgy in your future, that's all."

Is she suggesting that I have a thing for George? Oh, come on. He's a nice guy and everything, but he's nowhere near as cute as Nathan or Aubrey. Not that cuteness is the deciding factor or anything, but it definitely helps. Even a nun would admit that. Well, maybe. They're probably more into cleanliness or something. Or, I guess, they wouldn't really be into anything, being a nun. Whatever.

"George and I are just friends."

"Uh-huh," she says again. Grrrr. Know-it-all cheerleaders.

Then Serena comes in after a perfunctory knock, and I tell

Lorelai I've got to go before she starts accusing me of wanting George's love child or something.

Serena drops her books on my bed and flops down. "You know someone named Lorelai?" she asks after I hang up. "That's so cutesy."

"Well, she is a cheerleader. I met her at the, um, orangutan sex talk."

She gives me a weird look. Well, who can blame her? I wish George had come up with something more mundane. Like a talk on Picasso or something.

"Seems like a lot of people go to these talks."

I've used the parent excuse already. I have to think of another one for Lorelai. "I think she volunteers at the museum and gets extra credit or something. Anyway, how's your paper going?"

I guess Serena buys it since she pulls out her stuff, and we get to work. I hate lying to her, but what else can I do? Maybe it will be easier to hide once I've actually turned, and I won't have to be attending these stupid vampire lessons anymore.

Wow, I actually thought "when" there instead of "if." Is that like a Freudian thing? Have I actually made up my mind? Have to think more on this later after Serena is gone.

We work until Mom calls us to come eat dinner. Spaghetti

157

and meatballs. Good thing Serena isn't wearing her new dress. Dad asks us how school is going (fine) and what we're learning these days (not much, especially on my part, but it's not like I don't have an excuse), and whether we're excited about being juniors about to become seniors. (I haven't even thought about it.) Mom asks whether we've thought about prom yet (uh, yeah) and do we know what we want to wear (not a clue) and any idea who we'll be going with (wish I knew).

We help Mom with the dishes while Dad wanders back to the living room, probably to watch some boring documentary on some dead guy.

"How are your studies going, Serena?"

"Fine, Mrs. H. I'm just glad my mom doesn't make me go to those weird lectures you're making Mina go to!"

Mom, of course, is totally like "Huh?" so I jump in quickly with: "There're worse ways to spend my *Tuesdays* and *Thursdays*. They could be making me clean out the basement."

"Oh," says Mom. "Well, we just hope Mina is getting something out of the, um, lectures."

"Very cultural," I say sagely.

Another disaster averted by the lightning mind of me, Mina Hamilton. Though, of course, I'll have to explain some stuff to Mom later on. I may leave out the whole orangutan sex part though.

Serena and I head back to my room to do a little more dissection on the old Count. Or would that be vivisection?

I'm puzzling through a passage particularly thick with Van Helsing's stupid accent (what exactly was Stoker thinking?) when I hear Serena let out a big sigh.

"I wish I were a vampire," she says.

Say what? "Why?" I can't imagine how this book would make anyone want to be one. Though the women vampires are kind of voluptuous and sexy. But then there's the whole evil thing. They *eat* children.

"Well, not like the Count." Whew. "More like from *Interview with a Vampire* or *Ultraviolet*. It would be so cool to be able to travel everywhere and live so long you could see *everything*. Never running out of time."

I can see how that would be important to someone who's always late to everything.

"What about the whole bloodsucking part?"

Serena makes a face. My feelings exactly. It's one of the biggest things still giving me pause. I did, after all, nearly throw up my first time in a blood bar.

"Yeah, I can't imagine sucking on someone's neck. There'd have to be some way to work around that. That part is kind of gross."

That would be the blood bars and blood mini-marts, but I don't bring them up. What would Serena say if I did? Would she be grossed out? Intrigued? God, I can't believe I can't talk about this with her.

"So you'd really do it if you could?"

"Yeah, if vampires were real," she says. "In a minute."

That's just great. My best friend in the whole world:

a) Doesn't even believe in vampires, but would be one if she could.

b) Would have no problem whatsoever making the hardest decision in my life, the one that is keeping me up nights and giving me nightmares about Uncle Mortie bellying up to the bar and giant, nonexistent bats.

c) Might even turn with me, if she could.

But the worst thing is, I can't talk to her about any of this.

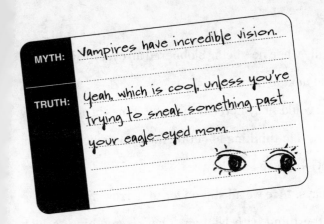

MYTH:	Vampires have incredible vision.
TRUTH:	Yeah, which is cool, unless you're trying to sneak something past your eagle-eyed mom.

15

All day long I can't stop thinking about what Serena said while we were studying last night. How come she's so positive she'd do it, but I'm still waffling back and forth? I mean, I'm positive I'm going to do it one minute and then the next minute I'm just not sure. I'm still pissed they're making me choose so quickly. Life-changing decisions should come with different time frames than normal decisions. This one should be at least a six monther. Maybe even a year. Maybe longer. After all, once you turn, you've got all the time in the world.

George and I are once again the first ones at the session, which I'm sure will give Lorelai something to comment about. I briefly consider not sitting next to him but then figure that's just stupid. I enjoy his company, and who cares what anybody thinks anyway? And besides, I can't say that I'm really fond of Aubrey lately, especially when he's being slobbered all over by Raven. I'm not about to sit next to him.

Of course, I could sit by Lorelai when she comes in or by freaky Linda. I suspect I'm thinking about this way too much. I just sit down next to George and say hey.

"Hey," he says. "Are we all still on for tomorrow night?"

Oh yeah, the thing with Nathan. That's something to look forward to. "As far as I know. You sure you want to go? It might be boring. I'm not sure what we're going to do."

"I don't have anything else planned. And I can't think of anyone else I'd rather spend time with than you guys."

See, that was nice. He's such a nice guy.

"I think you'll like Nathan okay. He's really cool." I'm starting to think that maybe, just maybe, Serena had a great idea. It'll be like a double date instead of just a friendly gang. I can totally see Serena and George hooking up, which would make my going out with Nathan even better. I always hated it when I had a boyfriend and Serena didn't and vice versa. Not that it happened all that often, but still. You feel guilty going out when you know your best friend is sitting at home. And how awesome would it be if my two current BFs hit it off?

Lorelai comes in and gives me a knowing smile that I just ignore. She sits on my other side. Then Aubrey comes in *sans*

Raven and heads right over to me. Lorelai pretends to shuffle through her notebooks, and George just grunts and stares off into space. I need to ask him at some point what it is about Aubrey that he doesn't like.

"Hi Mina. Lorelai." I wait for him to include George, but he doesn't. That's just so testosterone.

"Aubrey," I say and just nod casually. "You remember George?"

"Oh, yeah. Hi, George." Aubrey looks a little uncomfortable for the first time since I've known him. George just nods and goes back to staring at the wall.

"Anyway, Mina, I was wondering if your uncle had anything else planned?"

Uncle Mortie? Oh, he must mean like the blood bar trip. "Probably. I'm not sure. I have to give him a call. He's not exactly reliable on remembering stuff like that."

"Oh. Well." Aubrey shoots a little bit of a nervous look at George again and then seems to regain his confidence. "Perhaps I could go with you and your uncle the next time? My sponsor is out of town for the next two weeks." He smiles, showing all his pearly whites.

I guess it wouldn't hurt. And he is drop-dead gorgeous. That doesn't hurt either. "I suppose so." Then it occurs to me that I should probably extend the invitation. "George? Lorelai? You

163

guys are welcome to come too. Uncle Mortie's usually a riot."

Aubrey's smile slips a little, but he says, "Great, thanks," and rushes off to find a seat before either George or Lorelai say anything.

"My sponsor is actually pretty good," says Lorelai. "But thanks for asking."

"How about you, George?"

"Actually, that would be nice. My sponsor isn't bad, but he is a little absentminded. He's pretty ancient. He's only taken me out to one of the hidden vampire museums so far. It was okay, but a little boring. Stakes that missed their mark, a collection of tombstones, vampire fashions through the ages, that kind of thing."

"Cool," I say, and Lorelai pokes me in the ribs and gives me another "I told you so" look. I ignore her.

Then Raven strolls through the door and right up to my desk without looking to the left or the right. She juts her chin out at me and puts her hands on her hips, like that's supposed to scare me.

"I thought I told you to stay away from Aubrey," she snarls.

Uh, newsflash, girlfriend. Aubrey's the one who's been coming over to me. I mean, who asked who if they could come over for dinner? But I don't say that. Instead, I just shrug and say, "It's a free world."

Mom says I'm a trouble magnet. If there's some kind of trouble brewing, chances are it will search me out and try to take me down with it. Dad says I just have a steel backbone and never back down. Me, I think that it's just that I can't stand stupid people. They annoy me.

So I'm waiting for Raven to make the first move. I'm pretty sure my casual answer will set her off, since people like her don't like their ultimatums to be ignored. And sure enough, she's puffing herself up like a blowfish ready to blow. I imagine she's not used to people challenging her in all her black-hearted Goth-ness. I stay seated and even pretend to look at my nails (hmmm, I need to put a new coat of polish on them) to show her just how little I care about her temper tantrum.

I know, I know. I should be more grown up. I'm technically almost an adult but I'm about to get into a fight with a Goth-girl over a boy I'm not even sure I like all that much. A really cute boy, but still. But Raven annoys the snot out of me, and I think I could take her. In fact, I'm positive I could. She's all makeup.

"You think you're so hot with your vampire relatives," she sneers at me. "But I'm going to turn soon and then we'll see who's hot. Then you'll just be another face in the crowd."

I give her a "whatever" look. She's not making any sense anyway.

165

"You'll just be nothing then." She continues, her finger stabbing dangerously close to my face. If it actually touches me, that's it. Go time. "And I know some of the Black Talons. So you had better watch your back." She's almost shouting by this time. Everyone in the room is staring at us, including Aubrey, who seems oblivious to being the cause of the problem.

Neither of us had noticed G.W. coming in until she lays a firm hand on Raven's shoulder and pulls her back a couple of feet away from me. Looking at her face, I'm glad I was the one sitting down and looking all innocent and not saying anything.

"Enough!" She gives Raven a shake, and the poor little Goth girl looks like a rag doll in her iron grip. "I don't ever want to hear that name in here again," she commands, looking right at Raven, who's looking just a wee bit terrified now. "Or another threat against a fellow candidate. Do you understand me?"

Raven manages to nod her head and Grandma Wolfington drops her like the piece of garbage she is. Goth girl stumbles a bit and then slinks over to an empty seat.

"I don't know what that was about and I don't want to know," says G.W., looking at me now. I stare back as innocently as I can. I'm not going to piss her off if I can help it. "But I expect to never hear of it again." I nod and I catch a glimpse of Raven doing the same from the corner of my eye.

Now I just need to find out who or what the Black Talons are. Not that I think Raven could really do anything. But you never know. It never hurts to be prepared.

"Okay, then." Grandma Wolfington claps her hands and everyone jumps and then sits at attention. Ha. I can bet there won't be any note-passing in class today. "Today we're going to be talking about health considerations and safety precautions that you should take as a vampire in the twenty-first century."

"We are not invulnerable to attack and some human diseases can also affect us, so it only makes sense that we stay informed and practice safe bloodletting."

If you think about it real hard, there's something almost kind of funny about that. Safe bloodletting. Isn't that like an oxymoron or something like that?

G.W. paces back and forth, probably still a little steamed from the Raven encounter. "AIDS," she says, so loudly that people jump again. "It won't kill us, but the HIV virus can severely impair our abilities. In some cases, it has been known to weaken us almost to the point of our prevampire state. In other words, we can become as weak as humans."

Interesting. I didn't know vampires could get diseases at all. But I guess it figures that if any disease would affect them, it would be AIDS.

"This isn't the middle ages anymore, where the worst thing you could get was a touch of the plague, which you could shake off in a week. The point is to know where the blood you're drinking is coming from."

She goes on for a while longer about other things to avoid like:

a) Excessive sunlight. Sun doesn't kill vampires like in the movies, but it can give you a killer headache because of your super-sensitive eyes. Not to mention a wicked sunburn, since your skin goes all pale because of some melanin-draining side effect of vampirism (the same reason your eyes turn blue or green).

b) Jumping off of tall buildings or other stupid MTV-ish stunts. You won't die, and you will heal after a while, but you'll be in a great deal of pain before you do. Plus, it brings attention to you that you don't want. You know, "Daredevil dude jumps off twenty-story building and survives!"

c) Crazy people with stakes or hatchets who fancy themselves to be vampire hunters. I think she just threw that one in to be funny.

She goes on and on about good places to get blood (Council-approved blood bars, blood-marts, known human sources—people who actually volunteer?) and bad places (fly-by-night blood bars, dark alleys). I don't know exactly how you're supposed to get blood from "known human sources." What, I'm just supposed to knock on Mrs. Finch's door and say, "Hey, can I borrow a cup of blood?"

George asks a question about blood types and whether there's any benefit to drinking one or the other (Just taste, she says. Ew.).

"And I don't want to hear about any Elizabeth Bathory copycats. Let me just say, once and for all, that bathing in blood has no effect whatsoever and will not sate your hunger."

Everyone around me is nodding their heads like they understand what she's talking about.

"Psssst," I stage whisper to George. "Who's this Bathory person?"

He doesn't even miss a beat in his note taking. "Romanian Countess from the 1500s. She liked to kill her chambermaids and bathe in their blood. Thought it made her look younger."

"She was a vampire?"

George snorts, which I take to mean, No, you silly girl, just a complete wacko, and turns back to listen to Grandma Wolfington.

Good heavens, am I really supposed to know stuff like this off the top of my head? Bloodthirsty countess trivia from the sixteenth century? Do fellow vampires come up and quiz you, or what? And bathing in blood? How gross! She certainly doesn't have to worry about *me* doing *that*.

By the end of the session, I've learned way more about blood and disease than I've ever wanted to know. There were a few other references to obscure historical figures I didn't recognize, but I wrote them down to look up later so I wouldn't look like an idiot. I wonder what Serena would think of all this stuff, if I could tell her about any of it. Would any of it change her mind or would she still want to be a bloodsucker?

I swear I'm going to quiz Uncle Mortie later. I bet that he has never heard of that stupid countess. And I'll ask him about the Black Talons too. Man, I'm getting quite a list of stuff to ask him. I still haven't gotten the complete scoop on his turning or what they do to you if you decide not to turn after they've let you in on all their secrets.

MYTH: Crosses repel vampires.

TRUTH: Who starts these rumors, anyway? The only thing that grosses my mom out is spiders, but she'll still step on one if my dad isn't around.

16

George has become a regular fixture at lunch and Serena definitely doesn't seem to mind it at all. They're going to make a totally cute couple. Tonight's little double-duty date is going to be awesome. Serena has been bubbling about it all day, and she even talked her mom into another new outfit. That's huge, since normally her mother saves all her money and attention for little Miss Prissy-Pants, Serena's little sister.

Alexis (with a name like that, she was doomed to be a spoiled brat) is only ten, but she's got her mom wrapped around her little finger. She competes in those stupid let's-objectify-females-as-much-as-we-can-while-they're-young-so-they-won't-think-twice-about-it-later beauty pageants and has won a fair amount of them. I personally think Serena started the whole Goth thing as an anti-Alexis move-ment, but it barely caused a blip on her mother's radar screen. She's a total pageant mom. All she'll talk about is how Alexis is going to win Miss America some day and won't that be special. Gag.

Serena's so jumpy about the whole date thing, she gets up halfway through lunch to go over to Nathan and reconfirm everything. And we never, and I mean never, cross over into the A-List's lunch area. Half the cafeteria goes quiet as she crosses the invisible line that separates us from them, but after she and Nathan start chatting each other up, everyone goes back to eating. (Or not-eating, in the case of the triple A's—Anorexia Addicts Anonymous. Sometimes I just want to go over to their table and shove some food down their throats.)

"So," says George, once Serena's gone over to A-List land, "what was the deal last night with you and Raven over Aubrey? Are you going out with him or something?"

"Nah," I say. I've been thinking about it. You add in personality to the list and Nathan wins, hands down. Aubrey just makes for good eye candy. "He's got the personality of a wet noodle."

George looks a little skeptical. "But why the big scene with Raven then? Why don't you just tell her you don't like him and be done with it?"

Yeah, I could do that. But what would be the fun? "I kind of like annoying the piss out of her," I say and give him a wink.

"Gotcha," he says. "I can see that. Just be careful. I wouldn't put anything past her."

172

Serena wanders back over with stars in her eyes and sits back down next to George with a humongous smile on her face.

"You could power lightbulbs with that smile." I tease her. "So, what's the scoop for tonight? I take it we're still on?"

"Oh, yeah." She smiles dreamily. "The plan is to hit Jill's party first and then go hang out at his place, just the four of us. His parents are out of town."

"Par-tay!" says George, in what I suspect is his sarcastic voice. Serena's too high on A-List fumes to notice.

"It's going to be great!" she says and pulls both of us into a group hug, no easy feat across the puke green cafeteria table. I haven't seen her this happy in eons.

I have Mom help me with my hair after school. I'm kind of hair-styling agnostic. It's not so much that I don't want to mess with my hair as it is that I'm just no good at it. If I were to try for a French twist, for instance, I'd wind up with something resembling a boa constrictor wrapped around my head. Mom insists on doing my hair whenever school photos are due.

Tonight she pulls it into a deceptively simple-looking twisted knot that looks both stylish and hip. I've got on a denim skirt made from two pairs of old jeans (Mom made it, not me), strappy heels, and a Bebe off-the-shoulder T-shirt with sparkles and glitter. If I do say so myself, I look totally hot.

I twirl around for Mom. "So, what do you think?"

"You look good, honey," she says. "Don't break any hearts."

I can't help myself. I let out a little giggle. No way am I breaking any hearts tonight. If Nathan wants a bit of a snuggle or a kiss, who am I to argue?

"Just remember," she adds, "you've got all the time in the world. Don't worry about moving too fast. I know how it is when you're a teenager and you just want to rush into things."

I give her a hug to reassure her that, yes, I'm a good, dutiful daughter and I'll take her advice to heart. And I will. She's got a point. If I do turn, there's no rush. But then again, I'm also not about to let Nathan get away when I've been lusting after him for years. I *wanna* reel this one in, baby. Especially since I don't know what'll happen between us if I do turn. But I'll worry about that later, as in after I've got him hook, line, and sinker.

Before Mom can give me any more Hallmark-card kind of advice, Serena and George arrive, all spiffed up. Serena's new flaming red tank mini is hot, hot, hot. Thank God Dad is out. He'd have a heart attack if he saw her. He still thinks of her as a little kid too.

George is a little more subdued, as per usual, but he looks pretty hot too. He's got on a green striped shirt that brings out the color in his eyes (how did I not notice they were green before?) and a pair of jeans that look well-worn and comfy. Obviously going for comfort over high fashion, but hey, it works for him.

Mom slips me a little extra cash (have I mentioned lately how cool my mom is?) on the way out, and we hit the town. Specifically, we hit the road for the long ride out to Jill's house. We all live in town, but Jill (and a lot of the A-listers, come to think of it) lives way out in suburbia in a fancy subdivision full of cutesy little hand-painted signs saying stuff like, "Please Keep Off the Grass" and "Thank You For Not Speeding," and every house is behind a big iron gate. Jill's is no exception, but the gate is open and the entire circular drive (which is huge) is packed with cars. And not just any kind of cars, we're talking Mercedes, BMWs, blah, blah, blah. Even if we had that kind of money, I don't think my parents would waste it buying me a fancy-schmancy car.

Serena's looking a little awed at the sight of all this obvious wealth. So I tickle her until she can't stop giggling and is gasping for breath. George looks on, grinning, but ignores Serena's pleas for backup. Good boy. Gotta train 'em early.

"Okay, okay, enough already! Stop before I mess up my hair!"

"Don't let them intimidate you," I tell her, "or I'll bring out the tickling fingers of death again." I wiggle my fingers at her and she backs up in mock horror. George laughs. It feels good, just the three of us hanging out and having a good time. But we all agree that it's time to face the top-40 music and head in, leaving the Death Beetle behind.

We knock, even though it seems totally unnecessary since people are milling around all over the lawn. Amazingly, Jill herself answers the door and looks blankly at us for a minute before snapping her fingers. "Ah, you guys are with Nathan, right?" We nod as a group. "I think he's in the kitchen, that way." She waves vaguely off to her left and then starts yelling at someone hanging off the fountain on the lawn. So we go on in and hang a left.

The inside is crawling with even more kids, and somehow the house looks even bigger on the inside than it did on the outside, which is amazing. I don't know what her parents do, but it obviously pays well. And speaking of parents, it's pretty obvious that there's not an adult in sight. I don't even recognize most of the kids, and some of them look suspiciously old, like college kids. Exactly what kind of college kids come to a high-school party anyway?

We find the kitchen after not too much wandering around. The kitchen alone is probably the size of my entire house. There are at least three refrigerators and an island you could sit the football team at. Thankfully, it's also a little less chaotic than the rest of the house. We also see the first adults, who happen to be frantic caterers busy filling tray after tray of goodies. Man. Rich people have it good.

Nathan is sitting on the counter strumming a guitar and humming along. You have to admit, he just keeps getting better and better the more I learn about him. Cute guy + guitar = potential rocking superstar babe. Guys *always* look better with a guitar. Forget that whole bringing a puppy to the park thing, just bring a guitar and I guarantee you a crowd of admiring girls. I push Aubrey even further back in my mind.

Speaking of a crowd of admiring girls, there's one gathered around Nathan right now. Including Bethany. Ugh. I've hated her ever since the third grade when she told the teacher I had a frog in my pocket. I got in trouble and had to let the frog go after I'd spent three hours trying to catch him. Okay, yes, I'd stuck gum in her hair first, but only because she'd made fun of Serena in her ballet costume.

We watch for a minute and then Bethany catches sight of us (in her compact, no less, as she was checking her lipstick).

"Oh, look who's here," she starts in a snippy voice until Nathan abruptly stops strumming. "The, uh, girls." She finishes lamely. Oh yeah, Nathan's got them trained, that's for sure.

He jumps off the counter in one fluid movement, dislodging his crowd of admirers and neatly missing a caterer passing by with a tray of itty-bitty sandwiches. "Serena-Mina!" he says and gives us a big hug. "And you must be George," he adds and gives him a hearty guy-thump on the back. "Nice to meet you. I've heard lots of good things about you." Hmm, I guess that means Serena's been talking George up to Nathan. I wonder what she said?

"How about we go out and sit in the gazebo?" The three of us nod and follow him out. Bethany and the others kind of hang back, not sure of what to do.

I've never actually seen a house with an actual gazebo before. I've only ever seen them in parks or zoos, things like that. But sure enough, Jill's got a big white gazebo with ivy growing up the sides in her backyard, along with a swimming pool, a cabana or two, and a Jacuzzi. A couple of stoners are out in the gazebo, but they get up and move on as soon as Nathan comes into view. What must it be like to have that kind of power? Where people just do what you want them to? Amazing. I wonder how he's escaped being a total spoiled brat.

Nathan sits in the middle of the gazebo with his guitar, and we sit sprawled around him. I make sure George is next to Serena. Maybe Nathan will play something romantic and love will be in the air.

"I thought we'd just take it easy back here for a while. The crowd scene isn't really my thing."

178

Huh. I thought that was a prereq for the leader of the pack. But it works for me. I'm not exactly into the scene back at the house. I like to actually be able to hear people when they talk to me.

"You know any Sleater-Kinney or Howie Day?" This from George, who I'd had pegged as more of a hard rock kind of guy.

"Yeah," says Nathan. "And Franz Ferdinand? You like them? Great for guitar."

They go off into a side discussion on guitar bands versus drum bands versus I don't know what while Serena and I look on helplessly. Okay, I like music and everything, but I'm not a walking iPod or anything. They finally settle on a band (one I've never even heard of) and start jamming. Nathan on the guitar and George providing rhythm with his hands and the wood bench built into the gazebo. And then George starts singing! I had no idea he could sing.

"He's got a great voice," Serena whispers to me.

"Yeah, I had no idea." George is a man of mystery and hidden talent. If Serena only knew the half of it.

The jam session actually draws a bit of a crowd, but no one else crowds our space in the gazebo. It's kind of cool, like being on the inside instead of on the outside looking in. Nathan and George don't even pretend to notice their audience and play on through a few more songs, none of which I'd ever heard before, but to which

George knows all the words. I hear a couple of girls in the crowd, thankfully *not* Bethany, ask each other "Hey, who's that guy?" and I know they aren't talking about Nathan. I start worrying about hustling him out of there before one of the vultures moves in on Serena's man. That is not part of the plan.

"You guys rock," I say when they pause for breath. "You're making me thirsty just watching you."

"I completely wasn't thinking," says Nathan apologetically (not exactly what I was going for, but it'll do). "I should have gotten you guys something to drink when we were back at the kitchen." He glances at his watch. "You want to just head on out to my place now? I've got stuff to drink and eat at my place."

Sounds kind of dangerous, but oh yeah am I ready to go. The four of us alone equals much more potential for make-out time. I jump up before Serena or George even reacts. "Sure, let's go!"

We bypass the house and walk around to the front. I spot Nathan's cute little Mini Cooper and head that way. "Okay if I catch a ride with you?"

"Sure," he says. "Serena drive you guys here?"

"Just call me James," Serena says. "As in, 'Home, James.' I'm Mina's dedicated driver."

"How come you don't have a car?" Nathan asks me.

I get that a lot. Sometimes I think I'm the only one at McAdam without one. It's me and Annabelle Mayflower, and she's morally opposed to supporting oil-rich countries or something like that. She bikes to school from like twelve miles away. All the freaks live in California.

"When I turned sixteen, my parents gave me a choice. I could either have a cheap-o car then or I could save the money and take a gap year after I graduate and go to Europe. So I picked Europe."

"Hell yeah!" says Nathan appreciatively.

My thoughts exactly. It kind of sucks not having a car, but I've been holding on to that dream of a trip to Europe. I'm planning on hitting at least three countries and doing my fair share of bistro-sitting, coffee-sipping, and cute-foreign-accent-guy-flirting. Hopefully none of this vampire business will have any effect on my plans. But I guess that will all be settled soon.

Okay, not thinking about that right now.

We make it to Nathan's house a little bit after ten, probably right around the time Jill's party really starts going strong. I know some of the seniors won't even show up until after midnight.

"My parents are on vacation, so we've got the whole place to ourselves." After Jill's house, Nathan's place seems like a quiet oasis. Much more my style.

He drops us off in the theater room (and yes, it's seriously a theater room with big plush velvet seats, a popcorn machine, and the biggest screen I've ever seen short of a movie theater) and says he'll be back in just a minute and to go ahead and start popping the popcorn if we want any.

"This place rocks," I say and plop down on one of the cushy chairs. I could totally get used to this.

"I told you," says Serena. "Just wait until you see the pool out back." She starts working on the popcorn machine and George wanders over to the shelves of DVDs to check out the titles.

By the time Nathan gets back with a cart (Just like a hotel! Well, not one I've actually been in, but I've at least heard of stuff like that.) full of goodies and drinks, the buttery smell of fresh popcorn has filled the room and George has a little pile of DVDs pulled out as possibles.

Nathan checks out his picks while we descend on the cart like a pack of vultures. Okay, maybe that's just me. Serena descends more like a dove. He's covered us on every angle—sodas (regular and diet), American beer (yuck—what dog piss would taste like if I were stupid enough to drink it), some English ale (I might try one later, who knows, maybe the English have better taste), wine (I have yet to develop that taste and right now, red wine reminds me a little too much of you-know-what), some virgin strawberry daiquiri mix (yum), and some harder stuff. And then there's the food. What, does he have a chef hidden in his kitchen? Actually, I guess that's not inconceivable in a place like this.

"*Kill Bill, Donnie Darko, Ferris Bueller's Day Off, Almost Famous, American Pie*, and *Fast Times at Ridgemont High*. Nice picks, George." I stop stuffing myself long enough to agree. Some of my favorites. Just add in a couple of chick flicks like *Sleepless in Seattle* and *Ten Things I Hate About You* (okay, I'm a closet girly-girl. There, I said it.) and you'd have my top picks.

We wind up watching *Kill Bill* first, and George and I act out the fight scenes, complete with goofy dialogue and weapons (a TV remote and a pencil). We probably look like total dorks, but it's fun and Nathan and Serena have a blast laughing at us. I just love Quentin Tarantino. His movies have awesome soundtracks, really cool visuals, and a lot of cheese, as in cheesiness. I challenge anyone to take *From Dusk Till Dawn* seriously. Even if you don't know anything about real vampires. I mean, come on.

Serena picks the next flick, which of course means *Donnie Darko* because:

a) She's got a total crush on Jake Gyllenhaal and even calls herself a Gyllenhaalic,

b) She loves obscure movies and you can't get any more obscure than *Donnie Darko*, and

c) She's into any movie with evil rabbits. And there aren't

183

that many of them, either, beyond *Donnie Darko* and *Monty Python and the Holy Grail*. That old movie, *Harvey*, has a giant invisible rabbit, but he wasn't evil, though it is kind of funny, so that's in Serena's list too. Have I mentioned that my best friend is a little weird? That's just the way I like her.

This time, it's Serena and George that do the play-by-play as Nathan and I crack up, though we do talk Serena into fast-forwarding through a couple of the slow parts. My only complaint is that the cushy movie chairs don't really allow for a lot of contact. Even though I'm sitting close enough to Nathan to smell his cologne (yummy woodsy spiceness), there's no way to just casually reach out and touch him without being really obvious.

It's pretty late by this time, so I give Mom a quick call to let her know that I'm not dead, but don't wait up for me any longer (which is kind of silly, as she doesn't actually sleep, but anyway) as I won't be home for a while, we're just having too good a time. She's cool about it, just reminds me one more time to be careful and gives me the obligatory Mom warning about the evils of drinking and driving.

I like being almost a senior. They've loosened the leash quite a bit in the last few months or so. As long as I call, they're cool if I stay out. Of course, if I came home puking drunk, I'm sure I'd get a severe talking to and be grounded until I was like thirty, but I've got no plans to do that.

Nathan gives us a tour of his McMansion, even the inner sanctum (his bedroom: blue walls, not too messy, lots of movie posters, and his own entertainment center complete with TV, stereo, and the latest gaming system). I see what Serena was talking about when we make it down to the pool. Whizz-bang! They could charge admission. Seriously.

Unlike Jill's pool, which is huge and rectangular (i.e., ostentatious but boring), Nathan's is all curved and blue lagoon–like with two waterfalls and a cute little bridge. One of the waterfalls is even big enough for two people to hang out behind. With all the tropical plants and mood lighting and the music softly playing out of hidden speakers, it's like being in paradise.

"I wish I'd brought my suit."

"No problem," says Nathan. "Just go in the tiki hut. We keep suits in all sizes in there for visitors." He looks me up and down. "Try the green one. I think that one would suit you."

Hmmm. I cross my fingers, hoping that the green one is a cute little two-piece and not one of those horrible things with a little skirt attached to it.

The green one turns out to be a one-piece, but it's kind of a sexy one with high-cut legs and a back that dips really low. It fits perfectly. I wonder if that means that Nathan has a good eye or has he been fantasizing about me so much he knows exactly what size I am? I hope it's the latter.

Serena picks another one-piece in red. Now that she's escaped the clutches of Goth-hood, she's embraced color completely. Nathan and George change too. (No Speedos, thank God—I've yet to see a guy that actually looks good in one and I'd also have to find something to look at when we talk because your eyes are inevitably drawn to where they shouldn't be. You just can't help it. It's like their crotches become magnets or something.)

We hang out in one of the smaller lagoons, which turns out to be a hot tub. No one says anything for a good twenty minutes as we just sit there and soak. The only sound is the bubbling of the water and the music (sounds like Morcheeba). Nice. Much better than a crazy party. There're probably people hanging from the chandeliers at Jill's place by now. If the chandeliers are still attached to the ceiling, that is.

Serena's the first one to break the silence. "This is so nice," she says. We all murmur agreement.

"Truth or Dare," George blurts out suddenly.

"For who?" asks Nathan.

"Anybody."

"I'll bite," says Serena. "Dare."

She's a brave girl, my Serena. Especially since the last time she took a dare she had to wear a pair of underwear on her head to school. Clean, of course.

"Okay . . . don't worry, I'll be nice." He thinks a minute. "Do a full on impression of your favorite singer." Funny. I figured he'd do the old standby of "give so-and-so a kiss" but I guess he can't do that when he's the one she should be kissing. That would be kind of self-serving.

Serena stands up and does her best Gwen Stefani with pouty lips and attitude, singing "I'm Just a Girl." She takes a bow and sits down a little out of breath when she's done. If she could actually sing, it would have been perfect.

"My turn now. Nathan. Truth or Dare?"

"Truth."

"Do you know who you're going to ask to prom?" Wow, she just goes right for the jugular. I kick her under the cover of the Jacuzzi bubbles. Not that I don't want to know, but still. Let's not be obvious or anything.

"Yep." He smiles at her.

"Well, who then?" she asks.

He wags his finger at her. "You're only allowed one question, you know." She groans. "Now it's my turn. How about you, George?"

"I'll take Dare," he says.

187

"Okay. I dare you to take Mina back behind the waterfall and kiss her." Say what? I do a double take. This was definitely not in the plan. What's he doing fobbing me off on someone else? Is this to throw me off the trail or what? Is he just testing me to see what I'll do?

Serena kicks me and I snap out of it and follow George over to the waterfall. You can't back out of a dare, even if it was someone else's.

George is waiting for me under there, sitting on a ledge. It's just as private and cozy as I imagined it would be. I pull myself up next to him.

"So . . . " I say, at a complete loss. I'm just not mentally prepared for this.

"We don't have to kiss, if you don't want to," he says. "I don't think they can see back here anyway." I look through the waterfall and see that he's right. I can only sort of make out their shapes in the hot tub through the water.

"No, that's okay. A dare is a dare. You don't have cooties or anything, do you?"

He laughs. "Not since I was five." Then he leans over fast, like he wants to just get it over with, but time slows down as soon as his lips touch mine. His kiss is soft and gentle like a butterfly fluttering against my lips. He tastes like strawberries (from the daiquiri, I guess). He finally pulls back until I can't even see his face. He clears his throat and then just hops in the water without saying a word and swims back to the hot tub.

Wow. George is a good kisser.

I sit there for just a second and then splash on over, hoping my face isn't blazing red. George looks perfectly calm, but he doesn't quite look me in the eye when I get back in.

"So, your turn, George," says Nathan.

I'd be the obvious next choice, but George says, "Why don't we play secrets and lies instead?"

"How do you play?"

"You have to tell a secret and then everyone guesses whether you told the truth or not."

"But how do we know if you really told the truth or not?" asks Serena, ever the practical one.

George just smiles and shrugs. "That's part of the fun."

"Ok," says Serena. "I'm game." Nathan and I agree. I'm a little relieved, actually. I'm not sure where the Truth or Dare game was going, but it sure wasn't where I'd expected.

"My secret is, I'm scared of making the wrong choice after high school and winding up alone forever." He looks at me now and gives me a little half-smile. I know he's not lying and when he says forever, he really means it. In fact, I know exactly what he means. At least my parents had each other. But how do I know if I'll find someone? What if I turn and wind up alone forever, sucking blood all by myself?

"Lie!" shouts Serena. "You know you're too nice a guy to end up that way."

"Lie," says Nathan. "You seem too together for that."

I debate about whether to say truth or not and decide to go along with the crowd, but still let George know I understand. "Lie," I say. "Because I know you won't make the wrong choice."

"Got me," he says and this time I know he's lying.

We take turns and learn a few things about one another:

a) Nathan hates cows and has ever since one stepped on him when he visited a farm on a school field trip. He once cheated on a test that he didn't prepare for.

b) Serena would like her sister to be kidnapped by wild dogs (I knew that). And she thinks emo is so over. Yet again more proof she's no Goth Girl.

c) George had a crush on his fifth-grade teacher and sent her anonymous love notes. And he once snuck into a movie theater to see an R-rated film, but wound up walking into the wrong theater and seeing a boring subtitled movie.

I don't give up too much on myself, just that I secretly wanted to be a ballerina until I actually tried on toe shoes and they pinched too much and that I'm afraid to dye my hair (what if it doesn't grow out right or it comes out purple or something?). We don't go back into real serious territory again.

It's kind of nice to know that George is freaked about his decision too. Sometimes I feel like I'm the only one. Lorelai is so gung ho (maybe it's a cheerleader thing, I don't know) and Raven, sheesh, she seems like she's been in training since she was five. Even Linda is committed.

Nathan walks us all out to the car and gives Serena and me a hug and George a healthy pounding on the back. "It's been fun hanging tonight," he says. "We'll have to do it again sometime."

Serena drops George off first and then heads on over to my house. "Too bad we didn't play Truth or Dare a little longer," she says as I get out of the car. "Who knows what could have happened."

"Yeah," I say and tell her goodnight. At least she doesn't seem mad about me kissing George. Yeesh. I can't believe I kissed *George*.

I can't believe how much I *liked* it either.

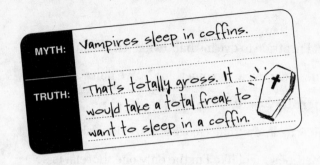

MYTH: Vampires sleep in coffins.

TRUTH: That's totally gross. It would take a total freak to want to sleep in a coffin.

17

Considering what time I went to sleep, I wake up amazingly early: 11 a.m. I brush my teeth and get a quick shower and then call Uncle Mortie to remind him of his sponsor duties, since I sort of invited George and Aubrey. Well, George anyway. Aubrey kind of invited himself.

He answers on the fourth ring with a "Yo!" I don't know what decade he thinks he's in, but it sure isn't this one.

"Hiya, Uncle Mortie. Just thought I'd check in with my favorite sponsor. See if you had anything planned for this weekend."

"Sure, kiddo," he says. "Didn't you get my note?" Yeah, like he really left a note. "I'll be there to pick you up in, oh, an hour or two."

Hopefully George is awake already, but it may not matter, since "an hour or two" to Uncle Mortie might add up to three or four.

"Would it be okay if a couple of my friends tag along?"

"From the vampire sessions?"

"Yep. Aubrey and George. You met Aubrey the other night at dinner." I cross my fingers. I don't think he was all that impressed with Aubrey when he met him.

"Ah," he says. "I suppose it would be okay."

"Great! You'll like George. He's got a great personality and an awesome sense of humor."

"Oh, so he must be the ugly one."

"What? No, he's not ugly. He's a normal-looking guy. He just really does have a great personality. Really."

"Uh-huh," says Uncle Mortie. "So he's not like that Aubrey character?"

Yeah, I knew he didn't get a good vibe from Aubrey. Well, I'm not so much anymore either, so I guess that's fair. "No, I think you'll like George."

"Ok," says Uncle Mortie. "But I'm not feeding them. Tell 'em to meet us at the Thistledown Café on the corner of Market and Eleventh Street. How about at three?" Heh. Yeah, I thought that "in an hour" thing was a little optimistic.

After I hang up with Uncle Un-hospitable, I ring Aubrey and George and give them the warning. George is miraculously awake and doing his laundry, but he said it could wait, he still had some clean underwear. I don't know how he does it all alone. Paying bills, making his own dinner, all of that. I give a silent thanks to Mom and Dad.

Uncle Mortie shows up reasonably close to on time and honks the horn until I climb in to the banana-mobile.

"Okay, Uncle Mortie," I say as soon as I get in, "It's pop quiz time."

"Alrighty, go ahead and shoot, kiddo" he replies and cracks his knuckles and his neck like they do in movies right before they go into fight. I totally want to learn how to do that. I can only manage a pitiful little snap. Maybe Uncle Mortie will teach me the trick someday.

"Number one: Why can't I just refuse to decide right now? What could The Council do anyway? Number two: What do they do to people who decide not to turn after they've been through all the sessions and everything? Number three: Who or what are the Black Talons? Number four: What's the real scoop on when you got turned? Number five: Do you know who Elizabeth Bathory was?" I think that's it. Somehow I get the feeling that I've missed one, but heck if I can remember what it is now.

"Geez, kiddo, that's enough. I'll start with the easy one. Elizabeth Bathory was a Romanian Countess. She liked to bathe in blood and killed hundreds of young chambermaids to get it."

194

I *cannot believe* he knew that. Oh man, I *am* going to have to remember this crap.

He must have seen the look on my face because he puts the car back in park and pats me on the arm. "Don't worry, nobody quizzes you on that stuff or anything. I only know it because that Riley woman gave me a way-too-detailed overview of the stuff you missed in the first sessions. I was supposed to clue you in on it, but I don't really see the use."

"Like Chemistry," I say. "I'm never going to use that in real life."

"You'd be surprised," he says cryptically and puts the car into drive and takes off, nearly running over Mrs. Finch. Good for him. She was probably just trying to get close enough to spy on us anyway.

"I'll tell you about my turning once we get back tonight. I need to not be driving for that one. Just remind me after we're alone again. As for the Black Talons . . . where did you hear about them, anyway?"

"This girl in Thursday's session. She wanted to kick my ass and threatened to sic the Black Talons on me."

"Oh, really," says Uncle Mortie. "We'll have to do something about that. Did you take her down?" Uncle Mortie knows I can kick some booty when I want to, unlike Dad, who would like to believe that I'm forever his little princess and wouldn't hurt a fly.

"I was going to, but Ms. Riley came in about then and broke it up."

"Well, the Black Talons are a small fringe faction among vampires. Pretty evil-minded, actually. They believe that vampires should rule the earth and that murdering humans left and right is perfectly acceptable. Do you think this girl really knows any of them?"

"I don't know for sure. She's a total wannabe, but I guess she could."

"I'll talk to Riley then." Uncle Mortie frowns. "And try not to kick the girl's ass for a while, just in case she really does have an in with them. They aren't exactly reasonable."

That's one of the things I like about Uncle Mortie. He doesn't tell me not to kick her ass, just to *try* not to. And he fully knows I could do it.

"As for ignoring The Council . . . don't even think about it. When they mean business, they mean business. I don't agree with them all the time, but you've got to follow along."

"Or what?"

"Or else."

"No, seriously, like what could they even do?"

Uncle Mortie actually pulls the car over and stops. He turns and looks me deep in the eyes. "The Council has a lot of power. They could make it very, very hard on your parents. And on you."

"Hard like what?"

"You're a stubborn kid," he says. "Like getting your parents fired from their jobs. Like making sure the IRS reviews their taxes every year. Or worse." He pulls back on the road again. "They've already fined your parents for having you in the house. So don't even think about not choosing."

"They've fined them? How much?" Uncle Mortie just looks at me. He probably wasn't even supposed to tell me that. "Alright, alright. I don't like it though." Blech. I guess I really have no choice. I don't want to be responsible for Dad losing his job or anything like that. That's just wrong they can push us around like that.

"I don't like it either, but that's just the way it is."

"Well, so what do they do to you if you decide not to turn after you've heard all the secrets?"

"They kill you."

"Say what??" My jaw drops somewhere near the vicinity of my ankles.

"Just kidding. You've heard about the Vampire Corps, right?"

"Yeah. Some insane woman came in and gave us the drill." I give Uncle Mortie a good smack on the arm for teasing me.

"Well, they have a special task force."

"That does what, follows you around to make sure you don't spill the beans?" That would suck. Like the vampire secret service or something.

Uncle Mortie chuckles. "No, they just erase your memories."

"They can do that? What, like all of them??"

"No, no, they try to just get the ones that deal with vampire stuff."

They "try" huh? That doesn't sound too good to me. What if they "try" and accidentally erase like all the memories of your birthday parties or something. Or everything you need to know to pass your Chemistry final?

"Yeah, but what would they do to me? I've known about the whole vampire thing since almost forever." It's not like they could just erase my whole memory of my family. Right?

"Well, they don't know how long you've known, but I'm not sure what would actually happen once the Corps got involved. But I can guarantee it probably wouldn't be pleasant," says Uncle Mortie.

Hmmm. I don't like the sound of that at all, not one bit. Maybe they would just erase everything. If they aren't above getting someone fired or, you know, some "safe" bloodletting, who's to say they'd mind leaving me brain dead? Or worse. .

We pull up at the café and George and Aubrey are already there, sitting on opposite sides of the place. Not like I expected them to be buddy-buddy, but I have to smile at the obvious testosterone-ness of it all.

I wave them over, and we take a table in the corner. Uncle Mortie treats us all to a café au lait. I knew he'd come through in the end.

"So, where're we going?" I forgot to ask him earlier. "What's the next stop on the vampire train of knowledge?"

"I'm taking you all to meet Harriet Melman."

That name sounds vaguely familiar, and I'm about to ask who the heck that is when both Aubrey and George go into some kind of weird fit, waving their hands around like crazy people and practically hyperventilating. What, is she some kind of porn star or something?

"I knew it," Aubrey exclaims. "I knew she had to be a real vampire!" Uncle Mortie and I shush him. Luckily there are only a few people in the café, and they look spaced out on espresso.

Uncle Mortie smiles like he's got a secret. But Aubrey doesn't seem to notice, and George is just repeating, "I can't believe it, I can't believe it," over and over with a crazy grin on his face. Who the heck is this woman?

I'm sure I'll look like a total idiot for not knowing, but I ask

Uncle Mortie anyway. It's not like I can go meet someone when I have no idea who she is.

"You've never read her books?" asks Uncle Mortie. Ah, so she's an author.

"What does she write?"

"Just some of the best vampire fiction ever!" George is practically jumping up and down. "I've read all of her books! I can't believe you've never read her! She's great!"

I have to grin; he's like a little kid pumped full of sugar or something. "I'm not really into horror novels," I explain. "I'm more of a mystery reader." Of course, I throw in an occasional romance novel too. I am a girl, after all.

"Harriet Melman inspired me to become a vampire," says Aubrey in a hushed, reverent tone. "I started reading her books when I was ten. I can't believe I'm going to meet her!" Oh yeah, that's where I heard the name before. When Aubrey was over for dinner sucking up to my parents. Heh. If Uncle Mortie's not careful, he's liable to get a group hug from the Harriet Melman fan society here. Aubrey practically has stars in his eyes.

"She lives just around the block," says Uncle Mortie. "I thought we'd just walk over." The guys jump up, practically knocking over the table in their rush to get to the door, completely leaving behind their half-empty coffee cups. I follow behind. I guess I'm just not all that excitable. I can't imagine getting that worked up about an author. Okay, maybe if we were going to meet Christian Bale or something.

Aubrey asks, "Does she really keep a boa constrictor?"

"She's got quite a few snakes," says Uncle Mortie.

"Is she really over six feet tall?"

"No, not quite."

"Does she really wear a purple turban?"

"Sometimes."

"Does she—"

"Okay, we're here!" Uncle Mortie interrupts with more than a little relief.

After the little impromptu Q&A session, I'm not sure what type of place I was expecting, but definitely something with more character than where we wind up. It looks just like every other house on the block.

Before Uncle Mortie can knock on the door, it swings open, reminding me of the blood bar. And behind it . . . the strangest looking person I've ever seen in my entire life, including the muscle-bound guy I once saw on the beach who had painted himself orange and was wearing a fez like you see on those guys in parades.

Harriet Melman isn't quite six feet, but she's definitely tall, and so thin that it makes her look even taller. She's wearing a humongous billowy purple dress that you can practically see through (that's how I could tell she's thin). Her hair is kind of pumpkin colored and sticking straight up on her head, like in cartoons when the character sticks his finger in a light socket. Her eyes are the weirdest thing, being almost violet colored (some funky contacts maybe?) and perfectly almond shaped. She's holding some kind of hairless animal (I have no idea what it is, but it is desperately ugly) and waving at us with her free hand (her three-inch long nails are painted black).

"Come in, come in," she purrs, and we all troop in, completely silent. I mean, what can you say to someone who looks like that? And talks like that. Are all authors this whacked?

Uncle Mortie smiles at her, ever the charmer, and kisses her hand. "Good to see you again, Harriet," he says. "This is my niece, Mina, and these are her friends George and Aubrey."

She smiles at us (Are her teeth pointed, or is that just my imagination?) and I give a little half curtsy. No way am I kissing her hand. George goes for a Japanese-style bow and Aubrey gives a little excited wave.

She puts down the hairless thing (what *is* that?), and it scampers off into the nether reaches of the house. I rip my eyes off of her and take my first real look at the place. If the outside was plain vanilla, the inside is somewhere between seventies

T.V.-style and the Matrix. There's crap *everywhere*.

She motions us to follow her down a dark hallway and we wind up in a circular room crammed full of even more stuff, including a coffin standing upright behind a couch. I opt for a perch on a leather chair with claw feet on the opposite side of the room from the coffin. Uncle Mortie sinks down into an overstuffed love-seat. George nearly disappears into a bean bag–type thing, and Aubrey sits daintily on the very edge of a rickety wooden chair that promptly collapses and dumps him on the floor. He doesn't get up (probably too embarrassed; I know I would be) and Harriet doesn't even seem to notice.

I think I've officially marked off "author" from my possible career choices. I could never be this weird. I may be a little odd, but I have never, ever seen anything like this. I wish Serena were here. She would be totally freaking.

"Would you care for something cold and refreshing?" I see Uncle Mortie give a quick shake of the head from the corner of my eye.

"No, thank you," I say before George or Aubrey can butt in. I'll trust Uncle Mortie on this one. He never turns down food without a good reason. "We just had some coffee."

She nods regally. "Lovely invention, coffee."

"Uh, yeah."

Dead silence as she sits and smiles at us.

"So," says Uncle Mortie, "Mina and the guys here are trying to decide whether or not to turn. I thought they might get a different perspective on things from you."

"Oh, definitely." She coos. "Not that I have anything against vampires, but I just don't see the point."

It takes a second for that to sink in for all of us and, quite frankly, I feel nothing but relief that she's *not* a vampire. This woman puts the freak into freakazoid. Aubrey, on the other hand, looks completely stunned.

"You're not . . . ?"

"Oh no," she says. "Silly boy."

"But, I thought . . . "

"I just write about them. Silly creatures." She leans forward conspiratorially. "Vampires are so tame now. All that talk about blood, blood, blood, but they've all forgotten about the thrill of the chase."

I raise my eyebrow at Uncle Mortie. So much for the whole Council edict about not letting outsiders in. Does *anyone* pay any attention to it? He just smiles at me.

"I suppose you could call me the unofficial advertising arm of the Vampire Clans. At least, for anyone crazy enough to believe the stuff I write." She laughs and Aubrey turns a nice healthy shade of red.

"So The Council knows you know about them then?" asks George.

"Oh, yes. They even periodically tell me some of the more interesting goings-on to try to get me to write about them. But it's usually much too boring to use. My books have to have drama! Suspense! Danger! Intrigue!"

Major freak alert. Harriet punctuates each word with a little jump and wiggle. Can you say weirdo? I just might have to pick up one of her books to see what all the Drama! Suspense! and Danger! is about.

George perseveres. "But I thought that The Council really didn't want to let any humans in on things and Ms. Riley specifically said they weren't exactly wanting to 'advertise' that vampires exist."

"Well, of course that's the official line. I happen to know that there are a few writers of vampire fiction that are in the know. And, of course, one particular one that *is* a vampire. But we don't talk about her." She sniffs. Hmmm. Must be her big competition.

"Why not?" Man, George is a total bloodhound.

She leans in close like she's about to impart something really momentous. "Because she's so *boring*, my dear. Always going on and on about the silliest things. B negative this, bad sunburns there, et cetera, et cetera." I can't help but laugh.

Aubrey finally spits out a question. "But what about all the stories you've written? I thought for sure that . . . that . . . " He trails off, doubtless remembering what she'd just said about the kind of people that would believe in the stuff she writes.

"Poor dear." She pats him on the head. "It's all just make-believe. You'll never find real life in a book."

George asks her some more questions about her books and characters while Aubrey sits there dead silent, looking like a little kid who's had his ice cream stolen. After a while, Uncle Mortie decides we've had enough adventure for one day and gives Harriet a friendly hug. Way closer than I would have gotten.

"It was lovely to see you again," he says, and she smiles at him playfully.

"Come again," she purrs to Uncle Mortie. I guess he's turned on the charm for her before. I wonder how they met. On second thought, I don't think I want to know.

"Uncle Mortie," I say as soon as we get outside, and punch him in the arm. "That was a dirty trick. You know we all thought she was a vampire."

He laughs. "I never said she was."

"I've gotta go," says Aubrey, and takes off at a near-run. We all look after him and allow ourselves a hearty laugh once he's out of earshot.

"I thought he was going to pee himself!"

"Maybe he did. Maybe that's why he had to go so fast." I know, I know, it's horrible. But we all had another good laugh at Aubrey's expense. I'm not sure what I ever saw in him. (Okay, that's a lie. The boy *is* hotter than hot.)

"So," I ask Uncle Mortie when we can talk again, "what exactly was the point of that?"

"I'm being a good sponsor," he says with a big grin. "Just trying to show you what all your options are. And teaching you not to believe everything you read."

I snort. "Options? Okay, let's see . . . " I tick them off on my fingers: "We can stay human with some or all of our memories erased or become a blood-sucking vampire and live forever. Hmmm."

George's radar goes off. "What's that about memory?"

"Oh, Uncle Mortie told me what they do to you if you decide not to turn after going through all the information sessions. They 'try' to erase all the vampire bits so you don't remember."

"Try?"

"Yeah, that's what he said."

"Really, kids," says Uncle Mortie. "I understand it's pretty foolproof. Not that I want to try it out. But I've never heard of any problems with it."

"Probably because anybody that had a problem with it can't

remember anything." I point out. Foolproof. Hah. Foolproof for the Vampire Goon Squad.

"True," says Uncle Mortie, which doesn't really make me feel any better. That's another way that he's not like most adults. He won't tell you something just to make you feel better. That's mostly good now, but it really sucked when I was five and still wanted to believe in the tooth fairy.

"Well," says George, "I better go. I need to go to work. But thanks for a really, uh . . . "

"—Interesting time!" I chime in with him. He gives me a shoulder squeeze and takes off.

"Nice guy," says Uncle Mortie.

"Yeah. I told you you'd like him."

"Much better than that wussy Aubrey kid. I don't know what you see in him."

I just nod. Better not to get into that kind of discussion with my uncle. I can just picture myself trying to explain why Aubrey's tight butt and soulful eyes were attractive to me. No way.

"So, what's the problem?"

"Huh?" What problem? I swear, the man likes to talk in riddles sometimes.

"Why aren't you going out with George? I can tell you're over the other kid, thank God."

Uh, hello? Just because you're related to someone does not make it automatically okay to comment on her social life. Really. "Because."

"Because what?" Obviously Uncle Mortie isn't taking the hint.

"Well, if you must know, I'm kind of seeing this guy Nathan at school. And I think Serena likes George. I'm going to fix them up. And I don't really think of George in that way. You know."

"Right," says Uncle Mortie, but he doesn't look convinced. What is it with people?

I decide it is well past time to change the subject. "So, the guys are gone now, are you finally going to tell me how you got turned?"

He sighs. Yeah, yeah, life is so hard. I give him a poke in his belly.

"All right. How about we go sit over in the park and I'll give you all the juicy details."

We settle into a bench and make sure no one is around to hear anything, being good little Council-abiding vampire citizens. Whatever. As far as I can tell, there's probably only like three people in town who don't know.

"It's not really that exciting of a story. Most of the details you know are true. I was out peddling vacuums and knocked on a door and met a woman. Her name is Madeleine." He pulls a grainy, dog-eared picture from his wallet. It's a picture of him leaning against his same old yellow Cadillac and a tiny little blonde woman standing next to him. They're both smiling big, wide happy smiles. She's pretty, with that whole vampire-glow, but not earth-shatteringly beautiful or anything. But I can see that she would have been a catch for Uncle Mortie back in the day.

"However, she didn't turn me right away, like you've probably always heard. She kept me for a few months."

"*Kept* you? Why? What for?"

"I was her love slave."

Uncle Mortie? A love slave? I stifle a laugh. I would never have imagined hearing that phrase in conjunction with my uncle. I mean, Uncle Mortie? He's not horrifically ugly or anything, but he's not exactly love-slave material, if you know what I mean. He's years older than my dad and looked then pretty much like he looks now—kinda balding, a bit of a pot belly, round face like Buddha or that Burger Boy restaurant guy. He's no Brad Pitt. Shoot, he's not even George Clooney. Turning helped things a bit, but he didn't have all that much to work with.

"Not all vampires toe the Council line when it comes to treatment of humans. There are groups that think humans should serve vampires, and we should be able to do whatever we want to with them. Madeleine is in that group, though she doesn't advocate violence, which was lucky for me."

Uncle Mortie puts the picture away and stares off into the distance. I decide not to interrupt with any snarky comments.

"I stayed with her for a while after she decided to turn me, and then I ran into your dad sort of by accident. He managed to snap me out of the spell I was in. Madeleine had a talent for mind control." He turns and looks me in the eye. "Don't ever think this vampire business isn't serious stuff. I know some of it seems a little silly and mundane sometimes, but there's a lot of history going back. Unscrupulous vampires can and do manipulate people all the time."

I nod without saying anything. Uncle Mortie sounds like he's on a roll, and I don't want to interrupt. Maybe he'll let loose on something really juicy. Of course, he did just tell me he was a love slave, but that's almost more gross than juicy.

"Before the early 1800s, there was no system of Councils. Everything was divided by clan and disputes often were ugly and vicious. It got to the point that vampires were in some danger of becoming extinct. Or at least quite rare. They were much more apt to kill humans and one another than to try and convert someone or get along. You've heard of Jack the Ripper?"

I nod again. Who hasn't heard of Jack the Ripper?

"Well, he was actually a fellow named James Maybrick and he was a vampire. That's the kind of attitude that prevailed back then. Vampires were their own worst enemies."

"Didn't he just disappear?"

"Not exactly. He was killed by fellow vampires afraid that he was becoming too obvious. That was around the time that the Councils started forming. A small group of vampires sought to bring some order to all of the bloodshed."

"So there's more than one Council?"

"Of course. There's The Northwest Regional Vampire Council that you're familiar with. Then the Northeast, Southwest, and Southeast in the rest of the United States. Then a bunch in Europe, Asia, Latin America—there's a Council for every area, basically. And then The Global Council. They rule over all the other Councils."

Blech. This is sounding way too much like that Government class I had to take back in the ninth grade. *Bo-ring* with a capital *B*. I figure I better redirect if I want to hear anything interesting.

"So, did you ever see Madeleine again?"

Uncle Mortie laughs so loud that a squirrel poking around nearby goes bounding off. "That's my girl," he says. "Forget the history and go for the spicy stuff." I smile a little sheepishly at him. I guess I need to work on not being quite so obvious.

"I've seen her once or twice at some vampire gatherings, but I've never really talked to her again. Afraid to, really. I thought I was really in love with her, but now I know better. I don't want to fall into that kind of trance again."

"Why didn't anyone ever tell me the whole story before? It's not that bad. It's not like you went on some killing spree or something like that."

"Well, I guess your parents just didn't want you to know before about the bad apples out there. And there is one more bit to the story. Your dad's conversion was kind of by accident. I'm not proud of it, but when he first pulled me away from Madeleine, I didn't hardly know who I was or where I was or anything. I bit him while he was trying to help me. And then your mom converted to be with him after she had you, but of course we couldn't convert you—you were a cute baby, but you wouldn't have wanted to be baby-shaped all your life, I imagine."

"Uh, no. Thanks for that."

"We stayed under The Council's radar for some time, otherwise I don't know what would have happened. They didn't learn about me until about twelve years ago and then your mom and dad were found out a couple of years after that. I'm afraid that was kind of my fault again. Your parents used a vampire contact of mine as a Realtor. He'd helped me get a deal on my house, and I'd thought he was a good guy. It turns out he turned your parents in when they didn't have the proper ID. Luckily, you were visiting your grandma at the time and we felt it best not to mention you. Let's just say that The Council wasn't real happy with any of us.

They wanted to move us around, split us up, and stuff like that, but your mom wouldn't back down."

"Ah," I say. Well, that explains why Uncle Mortie isn't exactly Mom's favorite relative and why I had to spend so much time at Grandma's back in the day. Though they could have warned me not to open the door to strange tax guys. That would have been useful info.

"Anyway, I think that's enough confession time for one day. How about I drop you off at home?"

"Sure," I say. Lord knows I've got enough stuff to think about. Like exactly what The Council is capable of doing.

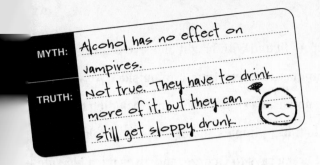

MYTH: Alcohol has no effect on vampires.

TRUTH: Not true. They have to drink more of it, but they can still get sloppy drunk.

18

Nathan actually comes and sits with Serena, George, and me at lunch for a while, until the restless clamoring of the A-List natives gets to be too much for him to ignore.

"Had a great time this weekend," he says, for like the third time and gives us a what-can-I-do shrug as he wanders back over to snotty land.

"Nice guy," says George.

"Oh, yeah." Serena and I say it in unison and then both blurt out "Jinx!" at the same time. George cracks up.

"You guys really are quite a pair. What are you going to do after . . . graduation?" I get the feeling that "graduation" wasn't what he was actually thinking about and I've been wondering the same thing. What am I going to do if I turn? How do I not let my best friend in on my little secret? She'd surely notice when I suddenly show up all fit and with bright blue eyes and suddenly I have to wear sunglasses every time I go outside. We've been close forever. She notices *everything* about me, including the stuff I'd rather she didn't, like pimples and crushes on stupid guys.

"We're BFF," Serena says to George, and gives me a big side hug. "Nothing will keep us apart!"

I don't say anything, but George gives me a sympathetic look. I guess it's a little easier for him. No parents or family to worry about, and no real best friends from foster-kid life. Not that any of that's a good thing. But it sure makes a life-changing decision a little easier when you don't have anyone to worry about other than yourself.

I'm still thinking about it on the way home with Serena. I can't imagine what my life would be like without her. I'd like to talk to Mom about it, but it's Girls' Night, which means Serena is staying over, so I won't have a chance to get Mom alone.

We've been doing Girls' Night once a month for years. We started doing it just to make sure to get Serena out of the house and away from her mother and little fright-night beauty queen Alexis. It used to be just on weekends, but once Mondays became rehash-the-weekend-beauty-pageant night, we moved it.

It's generally a lot of fun. We've tried on everything in my mom's closet before (current stuff equals yuck, but her older stuff is very retro) and concocted new hairstyles or makeup styles. The only stuff allowed is girly stuff. Have I mentioned I'm a closet girly-girl? Dad makes sure he's out of the house most of the night, and Mom sometimes invites over one of her friends too.

Tonight Mom's friend Rebecca is over. I've never actually figured out if Rebecca is a vampire or not and I've never bothered asking. She looks like she could be, but I'm not sure. Maybe she's just healthy. Her eyes are blue, but that's no guarantee either. It's not as if she talks incessantly about blood or anything.

Rebecca is a tad partial to wine and almost never has a boyfriend, so Girls' Nights with her tend to be slightly on the bitchy or hysterical side, depending on her intake. She looks to have gotten an early start today, but seems pretty jovial, though that can change at any moment.

"Girls!" she trills when we troop in. "Isn't it *prom* time? I brought magazines! And pictures!"

The pictures, of course, are of Rebecca's high school prom. She was actually pretty cute, but the dresses were absolutely hideous. When did people actually think that bows the size of your head were okay?

Mom drags out her pictures too, and I'm happy to say that her dress was moderately better than Rebecca's. At least it was a classic A-line.

"Do you know who you're going with, Mina? Serena?" Rebecca's dancing around the room with a couch pillow by this time. I'm guessing she's made inroads on bottle number two.

"No," we say in unison again.

"Well, better hurry up," says Rebecca, "or all the good ones will be taken. Do you at least have your eye on some potentials?"

"Yes," we say again. Serena adds, "but it isn't going to happen." I look at her in surprise. Did she already talk to George? I can't believe he wouldn't take her. He seems to like hanging out with us and everything and what's not to like about post-Goth Serena?

"Why not?" asks Mom.

"Oh, nothing," says Serena. "I just don't think the timing is right." Whatever that means. I'm going to have to talk to George tomorrow. Some guys just need a kick in the rear to get them going. Which reminds me, I need to do some serious hinting and Nathan-prodding myself.

We spend the rest of the night eating pizza and Oreos (not at the same time—that would be incredibly gross) and going through the magazines trying to find the perfect dress. I haven't been thinking about prom nearly as much as I should have, what with all the vampire stuff. One of the most important nights in my life is taking a definite backseat. I'll fix that starting tomorrow.

First a heart-to-heart with George and then I'll see when I can catch Nathan alone.

Mom makes Rebecca take the couch (she's in no shape to drive) and Serena and I hit the hay in my bedroom.

"You definitely have to get that red dress," I tell Serena. "I think you'd be stunning in it. I like that kind of retro paisley one for me. You think Nathan would like it?"

"Yeah," she says, "I'm sure it'll be fine." She yawns, a big classic Serena-style flycatcher. "I'm kind of tired now though, you mind if we don't talk anymore and just go to sleep?"

I agree. It has been a long day. Very unusual for Serena though. I usually have to wrestle her into submission before she goes to sleep. She's the original night owl. I'd have no idea what was going on in late night television if it wasn't for her.

WHY IT SUCKS TO BE ME, CONTINUED

1. It's getting harder and harder not to talk to Serena about all the stuff going on, and I can't see how it's going to get any better.

2. My parents are still keeping stuff from me. Why didn't they tell me The Council actually fined them? What else aren't they telling me? How come they trust me to make the biggest decision of my life, but they won't tell me everything that's going on?

3. And why hasn't Nathan asked me to the prom yet? Or at least on a date-date.

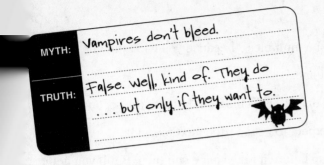

19

This time around, George, Lorelai, Linda, and I all arrive at the same time for the vampire lesson. We do our hellos and all sit next to one another in one corner of the room. Works for me, no place for Raven to sit and snipe at me. I'm trying to follow Uncle Mortie's advice and not get into an actual fight with her.

We're all pretty quiet, knowing this is one of our last sessions, until Linda, who barely ever even says a word, breaks the silence.

"Are you going to get a tattoo?" she blurts out to no one in particular.

Say what?! Just the mere fact that Linda (meek, mousy, Linda who looks like she might cry if you look at her funny) said the word "tattoo" is enough to wake all of us up. We all turn to stare at her, and she turns bright red.

"You know," she mumbles, "because you can't get one after. I think I might get one."

"You can't get one after?" This from Lorelai, the second-to-last person I would expect to get a tattoo next to Linda.

"No. It heals up before it takes once you turn. But if you get it before, it stays." Great. Yet another thing to decide in like a week. I'd toyed with the idea of getting a tattoo before, but now you'd really need to think about it. A tattoo for forever. You can't just get any old thing. I mean, can you imagine one of those cheesy tribal tattoos three hundred years from now? Or something that seems cool now but would look totally ridiculous later. Yeesh. Three hundred years. That freaks me out just to think about.

"So I guess you can't get it lasered off then either?" asks George. Huh. I wouldn't have thought he was a tattoo kind of guy either.

"Probably not."

"I don't think I'll be getting one then," says George. Yeah, me either. That's just too much pressure right now. And what if tattoos become really passé? It's bound to happen. Everything goes the way of the miniskirt sooner or later.

"I was thinking maybe I'd get just a little one. Like a bumblebee or something," says Linda. "Or a butterfly. Or maybe both."

"Cute," says Lorelai appreciatively. Linda beams. The girl seriously needs some friends or something. She's like a puppy dog.

"Why both?"

"You know, like Muhammed Ali. Float like a butterfly and sting like a bee?" Well. Yet another thing that I wasn't expecting to come out of Linda's mouth. Who knows what else is lurking in the hidden recesses of her mind. Next thing you know, she's going to tell us about how she does extreme sports in her off time.

Just as I'm getting a good image in my head of Linda on a half-pipe, Grandma Wolfington walks in. She wastes no time in getting started, even though a few people aren't there, including Aubrey.

"Today we're going to talk about what happens after you turn. You obviously can't expect to return to your life as it was before, so I'm going to be talking about how to leave your old life behind as safely and securely as possible with the least amount of disruption to not only yourself, but also to your friends and family."

Well, I guess this is a relevant session for once, since I just spent the last day or so wondering what to do about Serena. Though G.W. will probably keep her talk on the pro-turning track.

"Once you've turned, or perhaps even before, you'll be assigned a VRA agent. They'll come up with a plan for faking your death and creating your new identity. They'll also work with you to get all your affairs in order and the funds transferred to support your new life."

Say what?

I raise my hand to attract Grandma Wolfington's attention before she can move on to another topic. She nods at me to go ahead. "But my parents never did any of that when they turned."

"No, they didn't," says Grandma Wolfington darkly. "That was due to the unusual circumstances surrounding your uncle's turning and your father's conversion at his hand. However, old mistakes are now going to be rectified. Your parents have agreed to go along with The Council's recommendation and work with a VRA agent after these sessions are over, whether you decide to turn or not."

"What?"

"I assumed you knew. I suggest you talk to them about it once you are home," she says, and then goes back to the lesson as if she hadn't just completely turned my world upside down.

Hey, now, exactly how is it that *no one* bothered mentioning to me that, not only do I have to make the biggest decision of my entire life, but that I'd also have to give up everything and everyone I know if I do it? That if I turn, they're going to make me fake my death and move to who-knows-where? And what's that about them working with the VRA *no matter what*? Does that mean they'll be dead to me too if I don't turn? I mean, I'd know they were alive . . . or would I? Would they handily erase my memory? Would I think my parents were dead just like everyone else did?

I had planned on talking to George about the whole Serena-prom thing, but I'm not exactly in the mood for prom-talk. I rush out as soon as the session is over. Luckily or unluckily, I see that both Mom and Dad decided to pick me up tonight.

I get in the car and slam the door shut.

"Bad night?" asks Dad, and Mom turns around in her seat to look at me quizzically. I'm not normally a big tantrum thrower. But I think I've got just cause tonight.

"Exactly when were you going to tell me that they are forcing us to move and completely change our lives *and* we have to be dead too? Or deader. Officially. Whatever." I lost a little momentum there, but I think they got it.

"Ah," says Dad, his catchall phrase for conversations gone bad.

"And that I'd never get to see any of my friends ever again or possibly never see you again, depending on whether I turn or not."

"Well . . . " says Mom, her chosen method of delaying the inevitable.

"You guys didn't think this information just might be useful while making my decision? Just maybe? Just a little bit?" I can't remember the last time I was this mad. Maybe never. I would not be at all surprised if steam started coming out of my ears.

Mom and Dad look at each other while I glare at them from the backseat. I am so-o-o-o not letting them off the hook on this one.

"Well?" I manage to wring just a little more anger out of the word than normal. My old drama teacher would have been proud. She said I wasn't very convincing.

"We're sorry."

I can't believe it. "That's all you can say?"

"We don't have an excuse," says Dad. "I guess we just didn't want to unduly influence you one way or another, but we can see now that it was a bad choice."

"We're really sorry, honey," Mom adds.

I let out a huge breath and fall back against the seat. "Let's just go home. I have to think a minute." Dad starts driving without another word.

So, it basically comes down to losing my family or losing everything else. My friends. My home town. Everyone I know. My whole life. It was bad enough when I thought we'd have to maybe change neighborhoods. There's no way I could write to Serena after I was dead. I mean, what, letters from the beyond?

I can't imagine my life without her. But I can't imagine it without my family either. I'd be all alone and probably have no memory of them at all. Like George has been all these years.

I don't see how the Vampire Goon Squad could "condition" me otherwise.

All I can say is that this really, really sucks.

Hours later and I'm no closer to a solution than I was before. Morbid curiosity drives me to the Internet, where I look up the various ways a person can die. There's quite a few. You know, car wrecks, train wrecks, a horse falling on top of you, bad sushi, trying to be a hero in a bank robbery. Then my IM beeps.

9:33 P.M.

Luv&SqzMe: Mina?

MinaMonster: who're u?

Luv&SqzMe: George

MinaMonster: hey. wassup with ur scrn nm??

Luv&SqzMe: oh, like tht old bugs bunny
cartoon. hug & squeeze him n call
him george?

Luv&SqzMe: anywy, i got the feeling u weren't
paying much attention tonight in session

MinaMonster: u could say tht

Luv&SqzMe: yah, anywy, thought u might've
missed the homework assignment.

MinaMonster: homework?

Luv&SqzMe: y- make a list of pros and cons
  for turning. evryone has to do 1

MinaMonster: gr8.

Luv&SqzMe: anything i can help w/?

MinaMonster: no.

MinaMonster: thx tho

Luv&SqzMe: k call if u need something

MinaMonster: w8

MinaMonster: wht about prom?

The little prompt sits there blinking for so long that I think he must have left after all, but I figure I'll try again. Maybe he's just across the room and didn't hear the little ding.

MinaMonster: u going to ask s or wht?

I'm about to give up when his response finally appears.

Luv&SqzMe: u want me to?

MinaMonster: duh!! she's been w8ing!

Another long pause. What, has he got carpal tunnel all of a sudden?

Luv&SqzMe: OK

MinaMonster: gr8 thx got 2 go yell at the
'rents again

Luv&SqzMe: K, night

I stalk off to the living room, where Mom and Dad are watching another stupid documentary. Or trying to. They both look up as I come in the room. They've been waiting for me. I just know it.

"I just want to know one thing. And no excuses this time. I mean it. You owe me this much." I glare at them so they know I really mean business. "What do you guys want me to do?"

"I—" Dad looks at Mom, and she nods at him. She knows I mean it. "We, that is . . . We would like you to turn. We don't want to chance losing you." He lets out a big whoosh of breath like a weight has been lifted off of him.

"Thanks," I say and go back to my room. Might as well leave them hanging. It's not as if I know what I'm going to do yet anyway. These people are talking about my life here.

I decide to go ahead and do G.W.'s homework. Might as well. Maybe it'll actually help. The first item on both sides of my list is easy:

PROS	CONS
* Keep my family together.	* Never see any of my friends again. Especially Serena. Except George and Lorelai, I guess.
* Never have to eat broccoli again. Ever. Or liver. Or tofu.	
* Living essentially forever.	* Having to fake my death.
* Having super strength.	* Moving somewhere far away from here, since I can't exactly be seen walking around after I'm supposed to be dead.
* Never gaining weight, no matter what I eat. Ye-hah!	
* Never get my period again.	
* Picking out a new name and identity. (Actually, I don't know if this one is a plus or a minus. Could go either way.)	* Drinking blood. It even just sounds gross. Don't even get me started on those Coke and blood cocktails Uncle Mortie was telling me about.
* Not losing my memory.	
* Having to deal with idiots like Raven. But I guess people like Lorelai and George balance that out.	* Picking out a new name and identity.
* Looking young forever.	* Serena.

Serena is the thing I keep coming back to on the con side. The plusses outweigh the cons for the most part, as I kind of suspected. I guess I just have to decide whether or not my best friend or my family is more important. I wish I knew what I'd think thirty years from now. Or three hundred.

MYTH: Vampires live forever.

TRUTH: More or less.
Unless they run into
a stake.

20

I hardly sleep at all Tuesday night and by Wednesday morning, I feel like something has run me over. Something approximately the size of a semi and with the compassion of a bulldozer.

Serena is like a sister to me. Doesn't that count as family too? We know everything—well, like I said, *almost* everything— about each other. I've never even really kept a secret from her before. Okay, except for my parents being vampires. But other than that, nothing.

I can give up everything else, I guess, but I don't know how I can give up her.

I dig through my desk trying to find one of my favorite pictures from the time we went to the beach, just the two of us, for Spring Break. That was pretty much the best time ever, and we got one perfect picture of the two of us out of it. A once-in-a-lifetime picture where neither of us look fat, our hair is behaving, we're both smiling, and our eyes are open. I love that picture. So, of course, it's nowhere to be found. I think my old Mina-luck is back, if I ever even had any new-Mina-luck at all.

Then I remember that I'd e-mailed Serena a copy a couple of months ago. And since she never bothers to clean out her inbox, since the free storage limit is like ten giga-somethings, I'm pretty sure it will still be there. I sign into her e-mail account (seeing as we know everything about each other that includes things like passwords) and start looking for the message.

But the first message that catches my eye isn't from me to Serena. It's from Nathan. To Serena. Why would he have e-mailed her? Maybe he's wondering how to ask me to the prom? Trying to find out what my favorite color is?

I know I probably shouldn't open it, but I could really use some good news to cheer me up. So I click on it.

    hey S!

    what's up? had a rlly great time w/ you
    the other night. we have 2 do tht again. i
    never knew u were such a donnie darko fan,
    but i shld have known. :) tht movie is just
    as weird as u r! j/k.

233

```
anywy, i never get a chance to tlk to u
alone. so i thought i'd e-mail u. ok, i cld
have called but...i'm chicken... so, will u
go to prom w/ me? pls say yes & i'll make
sure u have an *awesome* time.

love, nate
```

Well.

Maybe it really wasn't such a good idea to read someone else's mail.

I can't believe Serena would do this to me! Why didn't she tell me that Nathan wanted to go to the prom with her? I click on her Sent Mail folder to see if I can find her response, and there it is, right on top.

```
Hi Nate,

i'd really, really love to go w/ you to the
prom, but i just can't. but thanks so much
for asking me. i'll always remember that.

sorry, serena
```

Oh ugh. Now I don't know whether I feel better or worse. So, let's recap, shall we?

a) Nathan doesn't like me the way I thought he did. Hoped he did. Whatever.

b) Nathan does like Serena.

c) Serena likes Nathan too. (Did you see that bit about "I'll always remember that"? Cheese.)

234

d) I am not going to the prom with Nathan.

e) Serena's not going to the prom with Nathan.

f) Oh crap! George is going to ask Serena to the prom because I am making him.

g) And in less than two weeks I have to decide what to do with the entire rest of my life.

I briefly debate just climbing back in bed and never getting out again, but now I've got at least two messes to clean up. One, I need to stop George from asking Serena to the prom. I do a quick check but he's not online. Shoot. That means I have to find him at school first. Hopefully he'll be all guy-like and put off asking her until late in the day. What in the world am I going to tell him? Ugh. Worry about that later.

Two, I need to find Nathan and tell him he's taking Serena to the prom. Yeah, I've been crushing on him forever and he is incredibly hot, but he obviously doesn't like me that way. And if anyone's going to have him, I'd rather it was Serena. And besides she was willing to give him up just for me? I feel like such sludge. How can I ever give up a best friend like that?

God, what if he asks someone like Bethany now? That would be a crime. I try to tell myself he wouldn't do that, he has too much taste. But you never know with guys. Sometimes they are swayed just by big tits. Not that Bethany is particularly blessed, but still. I've got to find him early enough in the day to make sure he doesn't do anything stupid.

As I'm getting into Serena's Death Beetle, it occurs to me that there's actually a Step One, Part A that I almost totally forgot. I don't want Serena to feel guilty about going to the prom with Nathan. I need to be the bigger friend here. The always-a-brides-maid-friend, but whatever.

"So, I've been thinking about prom some more," I say, almost too casually. Ugh. Gotta watch that or she'll know something is up.

"Yeah? You decide for sure on the paisley dress?"

"What? Oh, no, I meant about who I want to go with. I think I might ask that Aubrey guy after all. The one I was telling you about?" That's a total lie, but I hadn't had a chance to tell her what a jerk he turned out to be, so she should buy it.

Serena almost-but-not-quite swerves off the road as she turns to look at me. I pretend not to notice. "What about Nathan?" she asks.

"Nathan?" Here's where I've really got to play it cool. I shuffle around papers in my backpack like I'm looking for something. "He's nice enough and everything. And really cute. But the more I get to know him, the more I'm thinking maybe he's just not my type, you know? And that Aubrey guy is so hot. I bet Bethany will totally trip over her tongue when I walk in with him." I very carefully do not look directly at her.

"Oh."

I figure that's probably enough to at least spark her up, so I spend the rest of the trip chatting about the prom dress that I figure I won't even have a chance to wear, seeing as how all of my date prospects have dried up.

By third period I haven't seen either George or Nathan anywhere. I'm starting to get desperate. I definitely need to get to George before lunch. I pretend to have a coughing fit until Miss Perry gives me a hall pass and tells me to see the school nurse. Just in time too, since my throat is about to give out.

George has AP Calc third period, so I'm in luck for once. Mr. Davis has one of the few classrooms with two doors (one in front and one in back) and both of them have windows. I peek through the backdoor and see George. My luck is holding. He's only two rows away. I try to make just the tiniest bit of noise so Mr. Davis won't hear me but George will. I even wave frantically. George, of course, doesn't notice. It seems like he's totally engrossed in Calc. The nerd! But finally Martin Felder sees me and I pantomime to him to get George's attention. After two false starts (Martin seems to think me mouthing "George" sounds like "oar" and he makes paddling motions like I'm trying to ask him to go canoeing with me), George finally sees me and gets a bathroom pass.

"What's up?" he asks.

"You haven't asked Serena to the prom yet, have you?"

"No." He looks at me curiously. "I figured I'd do it at lunch, if that works for you."

I figure there's no way to do this easy without getting really embarrassing, so I just say it. "Don't ask her." I hope his feelings aren't hurt. I feel like a total Indian giver. Or asker. Not that I know any Indians and I'm sure they don't actually go around taking stuff back. Argh. Whatever.

"Ok," he says, looking confused, but not too wounded.

"Thanks," I say and give him a quick squeeze and take off for the library. Maybe the less said the better. Nathan's got study hall for third.

"Bye," George calls after me.

When I hit the library, I spy Nathan immediately sitting at a table over by the self-help section. But before I can head that way, Ms. Reed, the librarian and Study Hall Nazi, asks me what I'm doing.

"I, uh, need to look up something in a book." Yeah, I'm brilliant.

"Which book?"

Crap. I rack my brain for any kind of self help book that doesn't involve teenage sex. "That one, you know, about effective habits or something like that?" I vaguely remember Mom reading it when she went on a self-help kick.

"Ah," says Ms. Reed. "I think you mean *The 7 Habits of Highly Effective People*."

"Yes, that's it!"

"Okay," she says, satisfied. If there's one thing she likes better than catching someone doing something they aren't supposed to, it's figuring out what book you want. "You'll find that in the Self-Help section right over there. Would you like me to look up the catalog number for you?"

"No, that's okay. I'm sure I can find it." Whew. I jet over to the self-help section before she comes up with anything else to ask me.

Nathan gives me a little wave as I walk up. Luckily no one is sitting near enough to him to hear what is bound to be a completely mortifying discussion. I go over to the shelf right behind him and pretend I'm looking for that *7 Habits* book.

"Hey, Nathan," I whisper to him.

He sets his book upright. It covers the lower half of his face so Ms. Reed the Terrible can't see us talking. I can practically feel her beady eyes on my back. "What're you doing in the library?"

"I need to talk to you. About Serena." There's a part of me that just can't believe I'm about to do this. In the eighth grade I used to kiss Nathan's yearbook picture goodnight.

"Ok. What's up?" He sounds a little puzzled.

"You need to ask her to the prom again."

"She already said no."

I pick up a book and flip through it to make it look like I've found something. "She'll say yes this time."

"I don't know. Why'd she say no to begin with?"

Man. Why do guys have to make it so complicated? I try to think of a good story, but my brain comes up with nothing as I have apparently exhausted myself trying to think of the name of that self-help book. So I go with the truth.

"Because of me. She knew I liked you, so she turned you down. She didn't want to hurt my feelings."

Nathan almost turns around, but catches himself in time. I glance back at Ms. Reed, and she looks poised to get up at anytime.

"I didn't know you liked me," he says slowly.

"It's okay." I put the book down—it was something about being proud of your breasts or something—and pick up another one. "It's not your fault. But will you ask her again?"

"Sure. You sure she'll say yes?"

"Just don't take no for an answer," I say. "I know she likes you."

"Okay," he says and then adds, "Mina, I'm really sorry. I didn't mean to come between you guys or anything."

Ugh. See how decent he is? Does he not realize that actually makes this harder not easier? I will never understand guys.

"No problem," I say brightly. "I'll see you later!" I hightail it over to Ms. Reed and hand her the book I'd picked up before I embarrass myself any more than I already have.

"I decided to take this one instead," I say to her.

"*Surviving Teen Pregnancy: Your Choices, Dreams, and Decisions?*" Ms. Reed looks scandalized. Oh man, I should have looked at it before handing it to her. Now she's going to think I'm an ineffective pregnant slut. Why the heck do they even have that book in our library? I think only one girl got knocked up this year, and she wasn't exactly much of a reader, if you know what I mean.

"Uh, for a friend of mine," I say lamely.

She stamps the book and hands it back to me. "You know," she says in the nicest voice I've ever heard her use, "if you need someone to talk to . . ."

Oh Lord. Even Ms. Reed pities me. "Thanks," I say and grab the book, hoping she'll think my red cheeks are from gratitude. "I, um, have to get back to class." I run for the door and make it to the bathroom down the hall before I collapse. I hope Ms. Reed isn't much of a gossip. I hide the book in my locker and then go back to class.

WHY IT REALLY SUCKS TO BE ME

1. Nathan likes Serena. Really likes Serena. Likes Serena so much he asked her to the prom. And not me.

2. I'm probably not even going to the prom. So much for that sexy dress.

3. Serena didn't even tell me Nathan asked her, or that she likes Nathan. How could she do that? I tell her everything. Okay, almost everything. But she doesn't know that. As far as she knows, I tell her everything.

4. And George probably thinks I'm an idiot.

5. I am an idiot.

6. And the librarian thinks I'm pregnant. Like that's even possible. God, I hope she doesn't call my mom.

MYTH: Vampires can read minds.

TRUTH: Geez, I hope not. But it would explain some things about my mom.

21

It seems that the prom is on everyone's mind. As soon as I enter the community center for Thursday's vampire lesson, Lorelai pounces on me.

"Who are you going to prom with?"

"Nobody. I doubt if I'm even going to go."

"What?" Lorelai practically screeches. "What are you talking about? Of course you have to go! It's prom!"

"I don't have anybody to go with."

"What about Aubrey?"

I give her a look and she shrugs and moves right on. "Ok, what about that hottie you go to school with that you were telling me about?"

"He's going with my best friend Serena."

"Ouch." Yeah, I agree. But Serena's going to be so happy I

can't be mad. Well, not too mad. Depressed, maybe.

George and Linda come ambling up, talking some more about tattoos and kickboxing, from the sound of it. I will never get that girl.

"George!" yells Lorelai.

He jumps. Who can blame him? Sometimes I think cheerleaders forget how to converse at normal volume. To much "Yay, Team!" going on.

"Do you have a date for prom yet?"

"No," he says. I can see where Lorelai is heading with this, and she's going in a very embarrassing direction. He's going to think I made up that whole Serena thing as a smokescreen.

"Lorelai, I don't think . . . "

She completely ignores me. "Problem solved! You're taking Mina!"

George looks a bit confused. Or maybe "stunned" is the right word. Or maybe he's just creeped out and trying to be polite.

He looks at me, ignoring Lorelai. Serves her right. "Would you like to go to the prom with me, Mina?"

"I . . . " My first instinct is to say no. But then I think, why not? George is a great guy, and we're good friends. He's nice. He's not a mama's boy (which I guess would be impossible, considering) or an empty-headed jock (not that they're all emptyheaded, but sometimes when there's a stereotype, there's a reason). What would it hurt to go with him? We always have fun together. And I guess it's obvious now that Serena won't mind. "Yeah. I'd like to go with you. Why not?"

And the boy *can* kiss.

"Perfect," crows Lorelai. Then she grabs my arm and drags me over to a seat so I don't even get to see George's reaction. "Now, let's talk dresses."

I'd have probably been stuck discussing the benefits of long and slinky versus short and flouncey for days if G.W. hadn't come in. I never thought I'd be so glad to see Grandma Wolfington. I may be a closet girly-girl, but I can only take so much talk of hemlines.

"We've talked about the changes that will definitely happen to you after you've turned, but we haven't yet talked about what changes *might* happen. Some vampires experience additional changes to either their bodies or their capabilities, either immediately after their turning, or sometime thereafter."

Interesting. Hopefully she isn't talking about growing a third eye in the middle of your forehead or something gross like that.

"These changes can't be predicted or controlled, and most, if not all, of you will not experience them. However, I feel it is only fair to warn you about what might occur so you are completely prepared."

"What percentage of vampires experience these types of changes?" George asks.

"Generally, less than five percent. But we've had some time periods where as many as twenty percent of new recruits have abnormalities."

It sounds a bit less interesting when she calls them abnormalities. That definitely sounds like an extra appendage kind of thing. I am perfectly happy with the number of appendages I have, thank you very much.

"Most of the 'extra' changes that occur can be lumped into two categories: physical or mental. Physical abnormalities can include such things as X-ray vision, truly superhuman strength—or I guess I should say super-vampire strength—and changes in heat or cold sensitivity. The latter meaning that you would be able to tolerate much greater temperature ranges than normally possible."

Did she actually say X-ray vision? That's totally out of a comic book! But how cool would that be?

"Mental changes are less common, but include abilities commonly referred to as paranormal, such as extra-sensory perception or telekinesis."

I have always wanted to be telekinetic. How cool would it be to not have to walk across the room to get the TV remote or turn on a light?

Then Grandma Wolfington goes into her normal mode of way-too-much-detail, and I tune out. The woman could make anything boring, even a comedy routine. I sneak some looks at George dutifully filling out his notebook. I wonder if he's glad or not about the prom thing? He probably thinks I'm a total flake, since it was Lorelai that set the whole thing up—especially after I asked him to ask Serena to the prom and then demanded that he not. And it's not like I can explain that I'm *not* a total flake to him. You can't just go up to somebody and say, "Oh, by the way, I'm really not a total flake."

Then George catches me looking at him and gives me a half–smile, and I swing my focus back on Grandma Wolfington. Geez. You'd think I'd never seen a boy before. I should really get a grip on myself.

After the lecture, George comes up to me. I kind of expected him to, but was also kind of hoping that he wouldn't, since I was still (un)characteristically flustered. Okay, okay, I get flustered all the time, but still.

"I forgot to warn you," he says, "but prom will be the day after I turn. I was planning to turn right away since we'll be all done with these sessions. I've already set up a place with my sponsor. I don't think you knew that, so if you want to cancel, I'll understand. I don't even know what I'll look like."

247

So, there he is, being the polite gentleman and giving me a way out. Or does he want me to cancel because he doesn't want to go with me? Agh! I decide to take the chicken way out and make him make the choice.

"Oh, wow, big day. I'm fine, but I'd understand perfectly if you didn't want to go because of that. I mean, that's huge." I put as noncommitted a look on my face as possible. Now he's got an out if he wants. Ball in his court: Mina 1, George 0.

"Okay, great. I'll make the reservations and stuff then. And I was wondering if you wanted to maybe attend my turning too? I'd really like it if you were there." So I guess he doesn't want the out, which means he was just being nice. Or chicken like me.

"Absolutely, I wouldn't miss it." And I wouldn't. The one I saw with Uncle Mortie was pretty cool, but I didn't know that guy. I'm kind of curious how it'll be when it's someone important to me, which I guess he is.

George gives me the hundred-watt version of his smile and then leans over. I figure he's going to give me one of his quick hugs, so I step up, but instead he gives me a soft little kiss on the forehead.

"See you tomorrow at school," he says.

I just stare dumbly after him until Lorelai pokes me in the ribs and starts giving me the lowdown on her prom dress (a long slinky white silk dress with a slit up the side), dinner plans (romantic candlelit dinner at Le Jacques with her boyfriend), and the after party (some bash at someone's house I don't know and then the big debate over renting a hotel room or not renting a hotel room). It's another hour before I can get out of there, and I can still feel George's lips on my forehead. Weird.

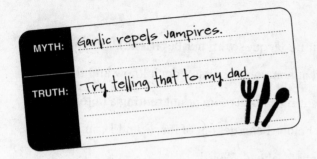

MYTH: Garlic repels vampires.

TRUTH: Try telling that to my dad.

22

Friday winds up pretty uneventful after Thursday's trauma-rama. I see George three times (in the hall between second and third period, at lunch, and before Ms. Tweeter's class) and he doesn't mention last night's forehead kiss *or* repeat it. Serena takes the news of me going with George to the prom perfectly in stride without a reaction whatsoever, which totally shocks me. What, did she never like him at all? We make a date to go dress shopping on the weekend since we are woefully behind in our prom prep. (Nathan did ask Serena again and she said yes.)

Serena drops me off at home with an admission that she's going out with Nathan on a date—a real date—tonight. She almost looks embarrassed. I play the good friend.

"Great! Sneak a picture and e-mail it to me so I can see how hot you two look out on the town!"

She has no idea how good of a friend I really am, but I'm not about to tell her.

I figure this calls for at least a bowl full of ice cream, so I head into the kitchen but Dad stops me with my hand on the freezer door.

"No snacking tonight," he booms in his best dad voice. (Sometimes I swear he must practice.) "We're going out to eat!"

This is big news. We don't go out to eat very often. Since they don't have to eat, they don't even usually bother to cook every day. I mostly just cook for myself (Mom totally won't let me get by with just eating Pop-Tarts, which sucks), but it always seemed like a waste of money to eat out for them.

"What's the occasion?"

"Just that my baby girl is about to make the biggest decision of her life." He gives me a big hug and a sloppy kiss on my cheek. Cheese.

"We just thought it would be a nice family outing," Mom adds, coming into the kitchen wearing one of her best dresses. Dad's even wearing a suit.

"Wow. I guess I better change," I say. Mom and Dad smile big happy parent smiles at me and wave me up the stairs. I guess they're trying to make up for all the drama.

When I open the door to my bedroom, I see a present on the bed. Huh. They must feel *really* guilty. Well, I'm not one to not indulge my parents, so I figure I'll open it up.

I open the card first.

> *Dear Mina,*
>
> *We just wanted to let you know that we love you and that no matter what you choose, we will find some way to keep our family together.*
>
> > *Love,*
> > *Mom and Dad*
>
> *P.S. Don't worry, this isn't your birthday present. This is just a little something extra.*

I knew the P.S. must be from Mom. She'd know that would be one of my first thoughts. But my real first thought was more like, "Aaawwwwwwww." They really are great parents. But from what Uncle Mortie's said and Grandma Wolfington's threatened, I know that keeping the family together if I don't turn will not be an easy thing.

I open the box next. Inside is a totally bombshell Ella Moss dress. Score! I can't even remember the last time my parents picked out something for me that I would actually wear! I bet

252

my dad nearly had a fit when Mom brought it home (she had to have been the one to buy it—Dad's allergic to shopping) and saw the neckline, not to mention the price tag. They must really feel guilty.

I throw it on and freshen up my makeup (I actually did a decent job this morning, so it doesn't take too long) and waltz on downstairs.

Mom sees me first and gives me a big smile. "Do you like the dress?"

"Love it!" I give her a huge hug and Dad too, when he comes in the room. I can tell he's trying really, really hard not to say anything about the dress since he's looking everywhere but around my cleavage area. Which is just as well. I mean, he is my dad. I don't exactly want him scoping me out.

"So, where are we going?"

"I let your dad pick," says Mom.

Ah. That can mean only one thing: Italian. My dad is a sucker for garlic. That thing about vampires being driven away by garlic? Total fiction. He can't get enough of the stuff. The only thing that repels him is brussels sprouts, as far as I can tell.

"We're going to Strozzapreti's," he says proudly.

"Awesome!" Strozzapreti's is the one of the nicest Italian places in town. Dad's shelling out some big bucks tonight. Let me tell you, that's really rare. As an accountant, spending money is like his least favorite thing.

Strozzapreti's is pretty much exactly like I expected. Low lighting, a piano player playing Italian elevator music over in the corner, candles and flowers on every table, the works. Our waiter is even named Antonio.

"And what will the beautiful young lady be having tonight?" Man, if Aubrey had that accent on top of his looks, I might still be into him. Probably not, but maybe.

"I'll have the mushroom risotto, please." I just love mushrooms. Kind of like Dad and garlic, only not as bad with the aftereffects. I don't know how Mom can kiss Dad after an Italian meal. Especially with the whole super-sniffer thing.

After the waiter's gone, Dad reaches over and gives my hand a squeeze. "Mina, we meant what we said on the card," says Dad. "No matter what, we'll find a way."

"We really don't want to influence your decision," adds Mom.

"No offense," I interrupt, "but it's almost impossible for you guys to not influence me. I mean, you're my family." They both look a little down at that, like they've failed some big parent test. "But don't worry. I'll make the right choice for me. Promise."

That cheers them up a little, and when the main course gets there, Dad perks way up. By the time dessert arrives, he's in garlic heaven.

It's really nice having dinner with just the three of us. Dad's actually a pretty funny guy, once you get him to loosen up (wine does that pretty good; Mom's definitely doing the driving on the way back) and Mom can hold her own with a story. I know a lot of teenagers can't wait to get away from home after high school, but my parents just aren't that bad. I suppose I should be more angst-y, but I'm just not. They're pretty cool.

And they can make their canine teeth half an inch longer just by thinking about it. How many parents can do that? I used to think that was the coolest thing ever and I'd make Mom do it again and again. That's the one cheesy movie special effect that they've kind of got right. It's just totally cool.

I feel like I should take the weight off their shoulders and turn like they want me to. But it's not that easy. I just don't know what to do about Serena. I don't feel like I can ask them about it though. After all, think of all the things they've given up for me over the years.

MYTH: Holy water burns vampires.

TRUTH: That's just silly . . . it's water. Holy, but still.

23

The prom-dress shopping went amazingly well. Actually, I don't mind shopping in general; it's all usually good. Well, except for:

a) Bathing-suit shopping. And before someone starts beating me down, *yes*, I know I'm on the skinny side. But that doesn't make it any easier to buy a decent suit. Somehow I usually wind up with one that either squashes my breasts so flat I look like a twelve-year-old or I get those ever-so-attractive under the armpit breasts. You know what I mean.

b) Underwear shopping. It's not really so much the actual underwear that are the problem, but the fact that I always, and I mean every single time, run into some boy from school. It freaks me out that Tim Mathis knows what color my panties are. Of course, I could be asking *them* what the heck they are doing in women's lingerie, but I'm generally too busy trying to hide the lacy stuff before they get too good of a look.

c) SaveMart shopping. I'm not into the whole warehouse scene and those stupid little uniforms they make the employees wear? I'm embarrassed for them.

Anyway, I got a great dress even though the racks were mightily picked over. It's like a lime green, which sounds kind of gross but actually looks really good with my hair.

So you'd think everything would be picture-perfect, right? I've got a great dress, I've got a date (well, an escort, anyway), my best friend is über happy . . . but all I can think about is the fast approaching deadline (a dead . . . line . . . get it? Okay, so I suck at puns.) hanging over my head.

One minute I know what I'm going to do and the next minute I don't. Be a bloodsucker, don't be a bloodsucker. It's like a B movie gone bad in my head. See the amazing vampire girl! I spend literally all day Saturday, Sunday, and Monday going back and forth. I feel like a Ping Pong ball. Old life versus new life. Family versus best friend. Could Mom and Dad actually pull things off if I don't turn?

Serena even notices something is amiss through her happy-Nathan haze during our Monday night homework party.

She throws a pillow at me, whapping me right in the face.

"What's the matter with you, girl? I think you've read that same page like fifty times."

I put down my copy of *Dracula*. It certainly doesn't help with the whole big decision, let me tell you. "Probably more like sixty," I say.

"So, what's up? You haven't been yourself lately." She looks away from me for a minute. "Are you sure you aren't upset about me and Nathan?"

"Positive." I throw the pillow back at her and score a direct hit. "I'm really happy for you, you dog."

She grins back. "I'm so happy it's ridiculous."

"Tell me about it." I'd have thrown another pillow if I'd had one. It is really great to see her so happy, but also kind of annoying when I'm having such a crisis of my own.

"So . . . are you going to tell me what your problem is, or am I going to have to get it out of you the hard way?"

"The hard way being?"

"I'll think of something." She waves another pillow at me menacingly.

Normally, I'd be laughing when she did that. Normally, I'd have told her what my problem was ages ago, and I'd be feeling fine right now. Normally, I wouldn't have my whole life hanging in the balance. This time, I just sigh and look down at my book.

Serena throws a pillow at me. And then another one. And then launches herself and pins me down by the arms. She may be smaller and shorter, but never underestimate Serena when she's determined.

"Girl," she says in her best Uma Thurman as The Bride voice (which is actually pretty good, but was one thing that was definitely more effective when she was doing the Goth thing), "I am your best friend. You can tell me anything. Now. What is your problem?"

This, I suppose, is why The Council doesn't trust humans because I totally crack and unexpectedly break down and spill the whole sordid story: parents being vampires, having to choose, not knowing what to do, blah-de-blah-de-blah. Little violins playing in the background.

Serena lets my arms loose and rocks back on her heels. "Your *parents* are vampires?" She looks at me like I'm totally insane, which I am for telling her at all. "Bob? Marianne? No way." She picks up my copy of *Dracula* and pitches it across the room. "I think you've been studying too hard." It dawns on me that she doesn't believe me. This is not at all the reaction I thought she'd have.

"They are! And I have to decide whether or not I want to be one too. By the end of the week!" I should really, really shut up, but the look on her face is really ticking me off after I totally bared my

259

soul here. I mean, she's supposed to be my best friend and stick with me through thick and thin and all that. And believe me, even when I say things that sound totally crazy.

"Mina, seriously, you need to chill out and take a break from all this *Dracula* stuff."

"I *am* serious. Look at all this!" And I pull out all the crap I've been collecting from Grandma Wolfington and dump it on her lap.

She starts flipping through it with a completely dumbfounded look on her face. I start thinking about how I've completely screwed myself. If they have some of those vampire SWAT guys watching new recruits, I am so-o-o-o dead. I sneak a peek at the window, but I don't see anyone. I don't think. I pull the curtains anyway. G.W. *did* say she'd be watching me. What if she really meant it?

"Never mind," I say, and grab all the stuff back and throw it in my backpack again. "Just kidding. Ha, ha. Forget I said anything."

"Yeah, right," she says. "I know you. You *aren't* kidding, are you? Why didn't you tell me? How long have they been vampires?"

"Since forever," I say and flop backward, staring at the ceiling. So now she believes me. Figures.

"Forever? You mean like *forever* forever? Wow."

"Well, no, they aren't like that ancient or anything. Just since I was born. Well, Dad right before and Mom right after."

"Wow," she repeats. "So what's the issue? Why aren't you jumping up and down and saying 'Hell yes, I wanna live forever?'"

"You," I say. That's really what it comes down to.

"Me? What'd I do?"

"If I turn, we're all supposed to fake our deaths and move away and take on new identities."

"Yeah, but I know now. They, whoever 'they' are, can't do anything about that."

"Oh yeah they could. You don't know these people. Vampire SWAT Goons. They can do just about anything. They're like the NSA or the FBI or the CIA. But with fangs."

"Mina," she says, "has anyone ever been able to keep us apart before? You do your turning thing or whatever you call it. I'll cry buckets at your funeral, we'll lay low for a while, and then you write me with your new identity. They can't watch you forever."

"Well, technically, they could." I mean, they are vampires. Forever is a relative thing.

She snorts. "Do you honestly think they're going to permanently assign like a secret service agent to you or something? Get real. I love you, but you're not that important. Besides, you're going on your big European jaunt after senior year and I'm going right to

261

UC Berkeley or UC Davis. We always knew we'd have some time apart, but that doesn't mean we have to *always* be apart."

Then I get a brainstorm. Why didn't I think of this before? "Why don't you just turn too? Didn't you say you'd love to be a vampire just last week?"

She thinks about it for like a minute and then shakes her head. Obviously, she doesn't have the same decision-making problems I do. "A month ago, maybe. But now . . . "

"Nathan?"

"Yeah."

Can't argue with that. I might have been saying the same thing, if Nathan had actually been interested in me.

"You really think you can keep it a secret? And not tell anyone? And I mean anyone at all. 'Cause they will so swoop down and take your memory away if you do. They can do that, you know."

"I can do it," says Serena. "I'm a born actress. Didn't I make a great Lady Macbeth?"

"No comment."

Serena creams me with another pillow, which is exactly what I would have done if I were her.

"Thanks," I say, and she gives me a hug, since she knows I'm not talking about the pillow.

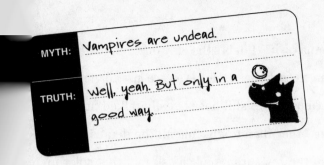

MYTH: Vampires are undead.

TRUTH: Well, yeah. But only in a good way.

24

Tuesday's vampire lesson (number seven for me, for anyone keeping track), is really the last lesson. After that, we're on our own. Well, us and those relocation specialists. No more Grandma Wolfington. Can't say that I'll be sorry to see her go.

Well, kind of. We almost all get to the session early, except for Aubrey, who's still missing (haven't seen him since the Melman fiasco), and Raven, who I'm sure wants to make a grand entrance. Everyone's pretty quiet. We're all thinking about the Big Decision. I swear you could light a bomb in the room, and no one would notice. Incidentally, what happens to a vampire if they get bombed? Not the over-drinking kind of bombed, but like a real bomb? Could you heal from that?

I guess it doesn't really matter. My prospects of getting blown up are pretty slim. Unless Raven ever learns how to make a bomb.

263

"Everyone gonna do it?" Linda's the only one that really looks more excited than overwhelmed. Her eyes are just all glowing.

"Yeah," says George. He still hasn't really talked about the whole prom thing other than to give me all the details like the time and name of the restaurant and to ask me what color my dress is. We're going to meet Nathan and Serena at a French place downtown before cruising over to the Hyatt Ballroom. Thank God there were enough funds this year so that the prom isn't being held in the gym.

"Oh yeah," says Lorelai. A few others just nod. I don't say anything. I still have my doubts and I'm just not ready to talk about it.

Linda pounces right on me for not saying anything.

"You aren't sure?" she asks. It's really more like an incredulous exclamation, like she can't believe anyone would even consider not doing it, like becoming a vampire is the best thing next to sliced bread, no-lick stamps, and iPods.

"Still thinking." I shrug.

G.W. click clacks up in a pair of two-inch heels, the sturdy librarian kind. "Alright, everyone," she says, "I've got a few announcements and some things to cover."

"We're still missing a couple of people." Linda volunteers. I'm sure she wants to make sure that everyone gets the chance to become the best thing on Earth.

Grandma Wolfington looks around with a sniff. "No, you're not," she says. "That will be covered in my announcements."

That little teaser makes everyone scamper into place and quiet right down. This has gotta be good.

True to her word, she doesn't waste any time or even make us wait to get to the good stuff. I could almost like her. Almost.

"Aubrey contacted me last week and he has decided not to proceed with turning, as may any of you, of course."

That brings out a startled gasp from everyone. If someone had asked me, I would have sworn he'd turn. But maybe Harriet Melman put the scare in him. I know she scared me.

"Did he say why?" I blurt out.

"Something about things not being what he expected. It seems he'd bought into some of the more outlandish myths, which is exactly why we have these sessions. At any rate, his situation has already been dealt with. I just wanted to let you know so that, if you happen to run into him, you'll be prepared when he doesn't remember you." That makes a few people do a little bit of a double take.

"What about Raven?" asks Linda.

Riley doesn't even look in Linda's direction or pretend to answer her question. "I'll be meeting with you one-on-one today. Starting with Lorelai." She points at the cheerleader, who blanches, and leads the way to the closet/office attached to the rec room we've spent so much time in.

"I wonder where Raven is?" says Linda plaintively.

"Obviously she doesn't want us to know," says George. "Can't say I miss her anyway."

I couldn't agree more, but it was really odd the way old Riley didn't even acknowledge the question. I wonder if Uncle Mortie did speak with her about our little tiff. Or is she just utterly ignoring Linda for some reason?

Lorelai comes out after a while with slightly more color in her face and sits down with a big whoosh. We all, of course, crowd around her (except for Linda, the next one up).

"It wasn't too bad," says Lorelai. "She just asked some questions. Nothing weird or anything like that. Just making sure we know what we want to do for real."

Oh. Well, I guess that isn't too bad. I was kind of expecting something more than that. I don't know what, just something.

My turn comes after Linda (who comes out just as cheerful as can be). I walk in and sit down. Somehow, she managed to stuff a desk and two chairs into the tiny room.

"Go ahead and sit down, Mina."

"Uncle Mortie says hey," I tell her. Not that he did. I just know it will bug her and I get a perverse pleasure out of doing that.

266

"Oh?" She attempts to smile. "How nice." Hehehe. "So, my first question to you is whether you have decided what you would like to do?"

Well, let's just get right to the point then, shall we? "I think so."

"You think so?"

"Yes," I say with as much conviction as I can muster. "I've made my decision."

She nods. I guess I pass the first test. I figure the next question will be what my decision is, but she surprises me.

"Why?"

Why? Why what? I can't imagine she means why did I decide—duh, because you *made* me. "You mean why I chose what I chose?"

"Yes. What made you decide on the path you have chosen?"

Lots of things go through my head, but I definitely can't mention any of the Serena pieces.

"Because it's right for me," I finally say. That's the most honest answer I can think of. Who knows, maybe she's got a lie detector power beyond the whole pulse-check thing. I wouldn't put it past her. She nods, smiles (a somewhat real one this time), and tells me I can go after giving me a session completion certificate (again, I have to ask, haven't these people ever heard the term "paper trail?") and another set of forms to fill out documenting

my decision and requesting Council sanction or some bureau-
cratic nonsense like that.

Before I do, I can't help but ask her one last question. "Did Uncle
Mortie say something to you about Raven and the Black Talons?
Is that why she's not here?"

She looks grim again. "He did speak with me, yes. And that,
among other reasons, is why she isn't here today. I'm afraid I can't
say anymore."

I nod. There're some things I'm probably better off not
knowing.

When I duck out of the little room, I see that Herr General (as
in the Vampire Corps Special Forces freak) has returned and is
talking to Linda earnestly over in the corner.

"What's up with that?" I ask George.

He shrugs his shoulders. "I think they're trying to recruit
Linda."

"Linda? As what? Cannon fodder?" Even though Linda did
manage to lose ten of the fifteen pounds she'd been lugging
around, she's by no means a lean, mean fighting machine.
I cannot picture her in army fatigues. But I guess vampires
wouldn't wear those anyway.

"Dunno. But she looks interested." True. Linda's still got that
big, goofy grin on her face. Well, if I ever run amuck, I guess

I'd be happy to meet up with Linda instead of someone like Grandma Wolfington. But you never know. Maybe she's really vicious underneath that girl-next-door image. She did have a killer handshake.

MYTH: Vampires have blue eyes.

TRUTH: Blue or green, actually. Dad and Uncle Mortie have blue, but Mom's are green. I wonder what George's will be?

25

Lucky for us, the teachers don't really bother to take attendance the Friday before prom. I'm glad I don't have to make up any excuses to tell Serena about why I'm not spending the day with her planning and replanning prom night. I just tell her it's George's turning day and come clean about the whole orangutan sex thing. I wish she could go, but that would totally blow our cover. She just makes me promise to give him a hug from her.

Uncle Mortie and Mom and Dad come along. (I think Mom and Dad want to check out my prom date, though Uncle Mortie already told them he likes him.) Other than that, Linda and Lorelai show up, Ms. Riley aka G.W., and a guy that I assume must be the weird friend that let him in on the secret, and a couple of other people I don't recognize. Not a ton of people.

George decided to go with a small ceremony in one of the

hidden vampire museums in the city instead of a big shindig at a blood bar. The museum is actually pretty cool. I wouldn't have minded if Uncle Mortie had taken me to one instead of visiting that kooky writer, but I guess then I would have missed out on seeing Aubrey practically cry over his misconceptions.

They have a whole collection of vampire writings, photos, art, all kinds of stuff. George's induction is being held in the Sixteenth-Century Room. There are period clothing pieces all along the walls. I'm so-o-o-o glad I wasn't alive then. I would never have put up with those dresses. And the lack of toilet paper, but that's another issue entirely.

George looks fairly calm, considering. He's chatting amiably with my dad and Uncle Mortie about his plans for the future, that kind of stuff, and even successfully fielding questions from Dad (argh!) on his plans for me and prom night. I tried telling Dad we were just going as friends, but he's got to pull the whole dad routine anyway. That's just how he is.

Then the light flickers a few times, and everyone gathers on one side of the room, leaving George and an older guy (Museum curator? Shaman doctor? Ancient vampire guy?) at the other end. The ceremony pretty much goes exactly like the last one I saw, except that George doesn't hesitate on his answer at all, and there's no chanting or dudes in robes and the old guy doesn't make quite so much a production out of the whole wrist-slitting thing. I'm proud of George. He looks strong and capable, like he knows what he's doing.

Once he drinks the blood the guy offers him (he didn't hesitate at all), his transformation is almost instantaneous. It's like he was blurry before and now he's come into focus. New muscles. His hair even seems to fall a little better. Nobody'd describe him as "just a guy" anymore, especially his eyes. They turn almost aquamarine.

I rush up to be first in line to give him a hug, but this couple steps right in front of me. I didn't even notice them before, and I can tell by the expression in George's face that he doesn't even know them. The bums. Probably museum visitors. They should have at least let friends go first.

"George," the strange guy says. "We're so proud of you."

"We've waited for this day for years," the woman adds.

"Do I know you?" George looks confused. I am too. They talk like he should know who the heck they are.

"We're your parents," says the guy and buries George in a huge bear hug.

I swear I nearly fall over, and George looks like he feels the same way. He stares at them both with his mouth wide open after the guy lets him out of the hug. Everyone is dead silent. The woman reaches out a tentative hand (guess she's not so gung ho as the guy) and touches George's arm.

"My parents are dead." George finally manages to get out.

"We turned, George. I'm so sorry. We wanted to take you with us, but the VRA wouldn't let us. You were too young. So we just watched over you as much as we could and nudged Tim into recruiting you when you were old enough."

Wow. So that's what would have happened to me if my parents hadn't hid me from The Council. Thank God they had the guts to do it. I could have grown up in an orphanage.

"You left me . . . to become vampires?" I can see George trying to get a handle on what's going on. I step up beside him so the absentee parents have to step back or get stepped on. I put an arm around his waist for support. I can't believe they're doing this to him right now.

"We didn't want to leave you. Please believe us. But they gave us no choice."

I just can't take it anymore. Who the hell do these people think they are? To come in here—today of all days—and expect him to roll over and play good son after not contacting him for years?

"What's wrong with you people? What, do you expect him to just give you a big hug and forget that you abandoned him?"

They look startled and a little guilty. That's exactly what they were expecting.

I glare at them. The nerve. "You want to leave, George?"

"Yeah," he says. "Yeah, I do." He turns to get his stuff and say thank you to the old guy who did the ceremony. (I've gotta say, he's got way more politeness in him than I do, especially considering the situation.)

I step closer to his parents and whisper-hiss at them so George can't hear. "And you did have a choice. Just ask my parents. They didn't abandon me. You only thought of yourselves." Then I grab George's arm, and we're out of there before anyone can say anything else or try to stop us.

"Where do you want to go?"

"Anywhere. Anywhere but here."

We hop in his car, and I drive (thank God Mom taught me how to drive a stick) around aimlessly for a while. George doesn't say anything at all. I wind up near the beach, so I park the car. It's a great place to think. The sound of the waves drowns out pretty much everything other than your own thoughts.

I pop some sunglasses on George so his newly sensitive eyes won't flip out and drag him down near the edge of the water. He doesn't bother taking off his shoes or anything, just sits down and stares at the waves.

"I can't believe it," he says. "They're still alive. All those years . . . " He takes my hand and squeezes it between both of his. I just squeeze back and don't complain about any squished fingers. "Did they ever think about what it must be like for me? All that time, just bouncing from one foster family to another? Some of them were bad. Really bad. How could they have done this to me?"

"I don't know." I can't think of anything else to say that wouldn't be stupid. I can't imagine how he feels or how they could have done what they did. This like tops the sucky cake.

My parents could have done the same thing to me. They could have been traveling the world all these years or whatever it was that George's parents have been doing. They gave up their lives for me. Sure, The Council finally caught up with them, but they aren't completely caving in to their demands. They'd fight for me if I didn't turn. They'd never just abandon me like George's parents did to him.

We sit there holding hands, not saying a word, until the sun goes all the way down. Then he drives me home and heads back to his apartment. I hope his parents aren't hiding out there.

Mom just asks me if George is okay when I come in. Doesn't say a word about how long we disappeared or how I didn't call or anything. I tell her I don't know, but he seems pretty messed up.

275

She nods, and I just go on up to bed. What else is there to do?

It isn't until around midnight that it occurs to me that we're supposed to go to the prom *tomorrow*. It seems kind of stupid now. I can't imagine that he'd want to go after the day he's had today. Poor George. It kind of depresses me to think of not going, but I've got to be a big girl and think of George first. It's not every day you find out your parents aren't dead, that they just abandoned you.

MYTH: Vampires are evil.

TRUTH: Stop believing everything you read!

26

I finally finish my *Dracula* paper. I needed something to do to keep my mind off of the whole George-prom-suckiness. Besides, it's due on Tuesday, the day before my project with Nathan (I don't know what Ms. Tweeter was thinking).

It isn't my best work (hey, I've been just a bit preoccupied), but it'll do. What I *really* want to write about is how unfairly vampires are portrayed in the book. I mean, they're all evil in there. But I bet if you told this story from the point of view of the Count, you'd get a whole different perspective. He's just trying to, you know, live or whatever you call it when you're undead, and gather a little family for company through all the long, long years. And then old Van Helsing has to go butting into things. And all these half-crazed guys digging up stuff and carrying on with torches and stakes and things. It's enough to drive any vampire crazy.

And so, in summary, I believe that Bram Stoker has done a real disservice not only to women, but also to vampires. Whereas the only compliment a woman receives (to Mina, from the all-knowing Van Helsing) throughout the whole book is that she has a "man's brain" and historically "womanly qualities" of reticence and humility fall to Lucy, a poor, pitiful excuse for a human being (who MUST be killed, once she obtains some semblance of self-confidence).

There's also Mr. Stoker's treatment of the female vampires. Described as wanton, lascivious, and in other lusty terms, Mr. Stoker is equating women's sexuality with evilness. Even Lucy is described in sexual terms once she has been turned, even though the girl had more suitors than she knew what to do with before she became a vampire. Poor Mina, however, isn't described as sexual at all, except when attacked by Dracula and held tight to his breast in her nightclothes. The rest of the time, she behaves practically like a man. And what does she get for that? She's left out of their confidence (almost to her doom). The men in this book plain don't trust women.

Only Dracula has respect for Mina, which is why he went after her. He also went after her to attack the men where it would hurt them the most, but have you ever wondered why all of his converts seem to be female? Well, other than the demented Renfield, but he was just a way in to get to Mina.

But I think that the most telling thing that Stoker refuses to recognize is the Count's desire for family. He takes care of the three women vampires as if they were his children (by feeding them kids, but still, it shows that he cares) and he admits to the men that he wants to convert Mina so that she will become part of his "family." Family is what's important in the end.

MYTH: Vampires have no reflection.

TRUTH: That's silly. How would you, check your makeup?

27

As soon as I can reasonably assume that Serena is awake—which is fairly early, considering it is the day of the prom and she's been in a tizzy all week—I give her a call to warn her that George and I are probably not going to go.

She wants to know if we got into a fight or if I did something stupid. (Hello? Thanks for the vote of confidence.) So I explain the whole thing, thankful at least that I don't have to lie anymore. I'd really be hard-pressed to explain things if she didn't know about the whole vampire situation.

"Wow," she says once I've got the whole story out.

"Yeah, wow," I say. It's like some crazy vampire soap opera or something. Next thing you know, Uncle Mortie's old flame will pop up or someone will discover they have an evil twin or go racing off a cliff in a tiny little sports car. Who knows.

"Well, you sure you don't want to go even if George doesn't? It's your prom too."

"I just wouldn't feel right. And besides, what am I going to do, sit around and watch you and Nathan swarm all over each other all night? I'll be fine."

"Okay, just call me if anything changes. Love ya."

I try calling George. No answer on either his home phone or his cell, which is pretty much what I expected. If I were him, I'd probably have pulled my phone out of the wall and shut off the cell.

I don't know what to do now. I'd had this whole day of prom prep planned, but it seems kind of useless now. I head over to the kitchen and put some cinnamon Pop-Tarts in the toaster. I could actually live off of these things, if Mom would let me.

Mom comes in to refill her coffee. "Heard anything from George today?"

"Nope."

"I'm sure he'll be fine, once he works it all out in his head. It's just such a shame." I nod and keep working on my Pop-Tart. They're best when you eat them piping hot.

"We talked with his parents for a little while."

"You did?" I snort in disapproval. The jerks. I'd be happy if I never saw them again.

"Yes. They aren't bad people, honey. At the time, they felt they had no other choice. They didn't have someone like your Uncle Mortie to egg them on, and they definitely weren't flying under the radar like your father and I were. We were lucky they didn't discover you years ago. I know that's no excuse, but try not to condemn them too much."

"Easy for you to say. George is a wreck."

"I'm sure he is. But, he may want to reach out to them some day."

"I doubt it."

"You never know. Anyway, what are you going to do about tonight?"

"Nothing. I don't want to be a third wheel with Serena and Nathan. Maybe I'll just totally veg out and watch sappy movies with you and Dad."

I head back to my room with another set of Pop-Tarts (Strawberry, with icing. In my opinion, it isn't a Pop-Tart if it doesn't have icing.) and try calling George again. Still no answer. I briefly consider going over to his place, but about the only thing he'd said to me on the drive home last night was that he just wanted some time alone to think.

Which you'd think would also mean don't call him, but I can't even take my own advice and dial his number at least twenty times before giving up. Just as well. I don't know what I'd say to him anyway. "I'm sorry" just really doesn't cut it in this situation.

By 5:45 p.m., I've got on my favorite pajama bottoms (light blue with little green bunnies) and one of Dad's old T-shirts (you can't beat an old T-shirt for sheer comfort), *Sleepless in Seattle* in the DVD player (which, of course, also means Mom and I have fresh tear tracks running down our faces), and a huge bowl of popcorn.

Mom's friend Rebecca is coming over (she not only owns *When Harry Met Sally* but also *10 Things I Hate About You, A Knight's Tale* and *An Affair to Remember*). Dad has agreed to keep us supplied with slice-and-bake cookies. He'll actually watch all the movies too, he just doesn't like to admit that he likes girly flicks.

When the doorbell rings, Mom just yells out for Rebecca to come on in. She waltzes in, movies in one hand and an unopened bottle of wine (surprise) in the other, and trills out "Oh looky here at what I found outside!"

George comes in right on her heels, all decked out in a dark gray tux with tails and carrying an iris corsage in his hand. He looks incredible.

"Uh, George," is the only thing I can think of to say.

He looks around, kind of confused. "Prom is tonight, right?"

Mom jumps up, hits pause on the remote, and grabs Rebecca.

"Mina," she says, "I'll plug in the curling iron. Go hop in your dress! Rebecca will do your makeup!" The two of them run off like a beauty pit crew.

I finally pry my jaw back up off of the floor. "I didn't think you'd want to go after yesterday. I tried calling . . . "

"Oh," he says. "I'm sorry. I unplugged the phone. You know . . . but I wouldn't miss prom with you for anything, Mina."

"Oh." I can feel a blush creeping up my face. "Um, well, do you mind waiting a minute?" I flee the room before he answers.

Mom is waiting with the dress, and she and Rebecca have me stripped, dressed, and in a chair before I have time to even think about what George just said.

"I have a prom date," I tell Mom.

"I know, honey. He's sitting in the living room. Now hold still so I can finish curling your hair."

"No, I mean I really have a prom *date*. Like a date-date."

"Of course you do!" Rebecca laughs, nearly jabbing out my eye with the mascara brush. "I saw that tux and those flowers. What did you think you had?"

"I dunno. I guess I thought we were kind of going as friends."

They both laugh at that. "Mina, you silly girl," says Rebecca, "no boy takes a girl to the prom just because they want to be friends."

Ah. Well, I guess someone could have told me that before. That would have been useful information. I didn't think George had that kind of interest in me.

Wow.

I have a date. A date-date. A *real* prom date. With George.

Ohmigod! I do a quick run around with my tongue to check for stray popcorn bits. It's too late to brush, they've already hit me with lipstick.

"Mints! I need a mint!" Rebecca shoves a mint in my mouth without missing a beat. In another three minutes, Mom turns off the curling iron, and they pull me up in front of a mirror.

"I'll go get the camera," Mom says and starts to run until she hears Dad from the living room yell back "I've already got the camera!"

It's amazing what two determined women can do in a short amount of time. Mom managed to curl and twirl my hair into this elaborate updo while Rebecca put on just the right amount of makeup (unlike her own style, which verges on hooker-in-a-slasher-flick). The dress is just perfect. A little retro, with one side falling all the way to the floor and the other has a slit up past my knee, so I can show a little leg.

I think I look okay. And judging by George's reaction when my makeup angels lead me back into the living room, he does too.

Dad makes him pin the corsage on me while he's taking a picture, and then Mom makes us pose in front of the house. Before they can catalog every step we make on the way to the car, I give Mom the okay-that's-enough-already look. And off we go.

"You look beautiful," says George.

"You too. Handsome, I mean."

And not another word is said until we get to the restaurant (amazingly on time—thank you Mom and Rebecca). I guess he's as freaked as I am, but at least he knew it was a date-date ahead of time. I must be an idiot, but I had no clue.

Serena and Nathan are already there, and she gives us both a huge hug, but doesn't say anything else. I don't want to get George involved in our little secret and definitely not Nathan.

"Hey, man," says Nathan. "You been working out or something?"

That makes Serena do a double take, and her eyes go a little wide. The whole turning thing was definitely a good move for George. He was all right before, nothing wrong or anything. But now he's really kind of hot. Hot *and* nice.

"Something like that," says George, and gives me a secret smile. I smile back.

Dinner is great (steak for the guys, extra rare for George, and seafood for the ladies), dessert even better (chocolate!), and prom . . . prom is out of this world. If I have to pick three highlights, it would be:

a) Seeing Bethany's face when I walk in with George, and Serena comes in with Nathan,

b) Finding out how good George smells during the slow dances, and

c) Having a real date-date with a guy who's also a great friend.

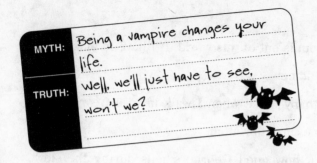

MYTH: Being a vampire changes your life.

TRUTH: Well, we'll just have to see, won't we?

28

Did I mention that the day after prom is my birthday, which makes this whole night just that much more special? George and I ring it in at the beach after midnight, walking through the waves (My heels in my hand, his coat on my shoulders, his socks and shoes off, and his trousers rolled up. And, of course, our arms around each other's waists.) Nathan and Serena decided to go for a long drive, and I can't say that I mind having George to myself.

We hadn't talked at all about the day before and the whole parent situation. I mostly hadn't brought it up because I didn't want to spoil the mood and it's not like I could have talked about it in front of Nathan anyway. But now's as good a time as any.

"Are you okay? With the whole parent thing?"

"Yeah," he says. "I don't really want to see them right now, but I know I have to sometime. They are my family. That's the important thing. But I'm going to give it a while."

I nod. He's right. Family is one of the most important things. Of course, the definition of family can also be stretched to include people that are important to you. Serena's been part of my family for years. And now George is too.

"You don't regret turning, do you?"

He looks surprised. "Why would I?"

"Well, you decided to turn partly because of the whole not-having-a-family thing. And now . . . "

"I don't regret it at all. Besides, I wouldn't have met you if it weren't for G.W. and those vampire sessions." Well, I can't argue with that. I just squeeze my arm around him a little tighter.

We find a nice little spot to sit and stare at the waves. George actually thought ahead enough to bring a blanket for us to sit down on. He puts his arm around my shoulders, and I lean against him. I'm remembering that Truth or Dare kiss (actually, can't get it out of my mind). We didn't really get in any major PDA time at prom. Ms. Reed had the evil eye on me the whole time.

"So"—I manage to get out—"how does it feel?"

"This? It feels great." He gives me a little squeeze and a soft kiss on the forehead. Definitely an A plus for an answer, but it wasn't what I meant. Though I did get a nice little wowee feeling in my stomach.

"No, I mean turning. Did it hurt at all?"

"Oh," he says and gives a little laugh (a 3.4 on the George scale). "No, it didn't hurt at all. It feels kind of good. But it's not really as quick as it looks. I'm still feeling changes inside of me. It's kind of a weird feeling, but not painful. Oh, but don't drink any carbonated beverages."

"Why?"

"Just don't. Trust me."

I laugh and sneak a little kiss on his cheek. I'm not quite brave enough to go for the lips yet, but I'm getting there.

"So," he says, "You've definitely decided, right?"

"Yep," I say.

"And?"

"And . . . hold on a sec, okay?" He nods. I use my cell to call Mom and Dad and tell 'em to get over to the beach as quick as they can and track down Uncle Mortie if possible.

"What are you up to?" At least he doesn't seem to mind the intrusion. It's not every girl that calls her parents to meet her and her date on the beach after prom.

"You'll see." I figure we've got a good ten or twenty minutes before they get here, so I decide to be brave. I lean over and kiss him. On the lips.

Oh man. That's all I can say.

Mom and Dad get there pretty darn quick (too quick) and Uncle Mortie gets there right on their heels.

"Everything okay?" That, of course, is Dad, ready to go all kung fu. I do a quick double check on George for lipstick, but there's nothing noticeable. Amazingly.

"Everything's great. I just wanted to get all the most important people in my life together. It's my birthday and I've made up my mind."

Dad looks a bit nervous, but everyone else seems pretty calm. George squeezes my hand. I can still feel him on my lips, and it is one good feeling, let me tell you.

I take a deep breath. "I'm going to do it," I say. "I can't imagine not being a blood-sucking night crawler with you guys."

We have hugs and laughs around. Dad looks very relieved, and Mom looks happier than I've seen her in ages.

"I knew you'd do it, kiddo," says Uncle Mortie.

"Actually," I say, "The real reason I called all you guys . . . Can I do it now? I mean, why wait, right? I'm not really into a whole Council-sanctioned event."

The adults confer for a minute and then Dad runs back to the car to get his coffee cup.

"It's not a golden chalice." He grins. "But it'll do."

I can't possibly play favorites and choose just one of them to donate the red stuff, so they all wind up putting a little of their blood in the cup. All the better, I think. If family is what got me into this mess, then it's only right that a little bit of each of them will see me through it. I only wish Serena could be here.

Dad hands me the cup, and they all stand back a little, but still close enough to touch. The only sounds I hear are the pounding of the waves on the shore and the beating of my heart. I may look calm on the outside, but my insides know better. But this is the right decision for me. I know it.

I close my eyes, hold my breath just in case, and lift the cup to my lips. No hesitation. At first, all I can taste is just warmth and then it spreads like fire throughout my body. It feels like waking up inside the sun; everything feels so alive. Not at all like I expected—I mean, after all, aren't I becoming one of the undead?

I feel like I could do anything, anything at all. When I open my eyes, I see my family staring back at me, and it's like seeing them for the first time. Now I can see every detail of them down to the tiny little laugh lines Uncle Mortie has around his eyes, the graceful way my mom moves, my dad's quiet strength, and George's beautiful smile.

"You know," I tell them, "This doesn't suck at all."

WHY IT ~~SUCKS~~ ^{Rocks} TO BE ME

1. I've got a boyfriend (not that we've formalized it or anything, but I'm pretty sure George wouldn't argue) who's seriously hot, seriously funny, and seriously nice.

2. And who can seriously kiss.

3. My best friend is as happy as I've ever seen her, and she's not willing to give up on me even though I'm officially a bloodsucker now.

4. I've got my whole life (death) ahead of me.

5. And my family and friends will be with me every step of the way (one way or another).

About the Author

Kimberly Pauley loves a good book she can sink her teeth into. As her alter-ego, the Young Adult Books Goddess of yabookscentral.com, she has devoured more books than she can count. This is her first novel. She lives in Illinois.

Pssst!

Hey, you! Yeah, you, the person who just finished reading about what happened to me when my parents decided I'd look better with fangs.

I bet you thought that was it, that now my life would be all perfect and happily-ever-after just like in all those fairy tales.

Well, let me tell you, that is *so* not my life. Or death. Whatever. Find out what happens next (you totally won't believe it, trust me) and why it...

-"MORE All-True Confessions of
MINA ~~HAMILTON~~ SMITH,
Teen Vampire

Kimberly Pauley

Coming September 2010

Turn the page for a sneak peek!

WHY IT STILL SUCKS TO BE ME

1. I finally get a boyfriend and a ~~life unlife?~~ death (ugh. whatever) and now he tells me we're going to be separated. For some undetermined-but-way-too-long-period-of-time. By like an entire ocean. Or whatever is between the United States and Brazil.

2. I totally suck at geography.

3. I have to leave behind my best friend Serena and change my name and all my stuff AND fake my death to move to Louisiana.

4. But not somewhere cool like New Orleans (ok, maybe I don't suck that bad at geography) where George could come visit me and we could do romantic date stuff and eat yummy beignets, but some small town in Louisiana.

5. No, not a small town. A teeny, tiny, miniscule itty-bitty-has-one-stoplight town where you probably can't even get a decent cup of espresso. What am I supposed to do there all night long? The whole no-sleeping thing as a vampire sucks bad enough here. It's bound to be a bazillion times worse there. Maybe a gazillion. That's bigger than a bazillon, isn't it?

6. Sure, my parents are so excited about how my dad gets to fulfill his lifelong dream of studying history or whatever (what is up with that, anyway?) with some famous creaky old vampire. But what about my dreams? Not that I know exactly what they are, but they sure didn't include getting stuck in the middle of nowhere with no friends and no boyfriend.

7. And, yeah, I love my mom, but I don't really need to bond with her in some stupid Council-sanctioned (i.e. probably sucky) class. Not even a shapeshifting one. Which, okay, does sound kind of cool. But with my mom??

But the absolute worst thing is that it's so totally unfair that here I am, some all-powerful (ha), all-knowing (yeah, right), in-control (totally not) vampire and my parents still get to dictate everything I do.

OPEN UP A WORLD OF ADVENTURE WITH THE

DUNGEONS & DRAGONS®

ROLEPLAYING GAME STARTER SET

RUN THE GAME
Build your own dungeons and pit your friends against monsters and villains!

PLAY THE GAME
Explore the dungeon with your friends, fight the monsters, and bring back the treasure!

GRAB SOME FRIENDS
AND THE
STARTER SET
AND
START PLAYING TODAY

playdnd.com